To that which we give the name
    is it ever less than divine?

In a space of mere hours, a life and faith in their entirety are to be re-lived by Simon Chance.

One-time missionary and bishop, Chance had withdrawn in mid-life to research – and teach – his enduring mentor Dante, creator of *The Divine Comedy*. He is recently widowed, after the prolonged descent into dementia of his devoted wife Marigold, violinist and composer.

To recuperate, he is invited by a life-long confidante, Clare, to her son's villa in the hills behind St Tropez in southern France, to join a house party of old friends from their university days, each now reaping the rewards of their worldly careers. The reunion coincides with the collapse of global banking confidence – and the playing-out of Clare's own loss of love.

But on a walk in the forest of the Massif des Maures surrounding the remote villa, in search of a church abandoned centuries ago, Chance loses his way – in a 'dark wood', as once experienced by Dante. The night turns wild.

Nor has Marigold been the only love of Simon Chance. The overwhelming liaison of his earlier life, pre-ordination, was with a student botanist. This very Evie, with her Parliamentarian spouse, is about to join the house party of Clare, her greatest friend.

A vital element in that searing, abandoned youthful liaison is yet to be reconciled which this scholar-cleric Chance has come to be. Now it rises to confront him. Here is the binding and defining weave of this night, unraveling in darkness, storm and dawn.

The working-through of the nature of love, physical and spiritual, in love's innocence and purity, will redeem Simon Chance or destroy him. Or both.

TOM STACEY (born 1930) has written fiction alongside his professions as newspaperman, publisher, penologist and ethnic campaigner. Starting young in Fleet Street, he was chief roving correspondent of the *Sunday Times* by the age of 30 and winner of the Foreign Correspondent of the Year award in 1961. As a newspaperman he reported from well over 120 countries, several repeatedly. His imprisonment in India (while covering the Kashmir issue) led to his involvement at home as a lifelong prison visitor and to his conception and devising (in 1981) of the electronic tag and to his championship of the tag as an alternative to jail and rehabilitative aid.

As a publisher from midlife, his imprints created comprehensive works on countries across the Middle East and the Islamic world, the 20- volume *Peoples of the Earth* series (co-published in 14 languages), and *The Concise Encyclopaedia of Islam*. His imprints' authors have backed or headed campaigns on counter-consensus issues.

His co-habiting with the peoples of the Ruwenzori Mountains on the Uganda-Congo border in 1954 gave rise to his major novel *The Brothers M* (1960, published in Britain, the US and in translation). Thereafter, his whole-hearted identification with the Rwenzururians' campaign for self-determination was vindicated by Uganda's ultimate recognition (2009) of the people and territory as a constitutional 'cultural' Kingdom in Uganda. In this his later book *Tribe, the Hidden History of the Mountains of the Moon* (2003) proved to have paid a decisive part.

He is a winner of the John Llewellyn Rhys Memorial Prize and a Fellow of the Royal Society of Literature.

Works by Tom Stacey

Novels
The Brothers M
The Living and the Dying
The Pandemonium
The Twelfth Night of Ramadan (under the nom de plume
Kendal J Peel)
The Worm of the Rose
Decline
The Man Who Knew Everything (first published as *Deadline*)

Collected Long Short Stories
Bodies and Souls

Separately Published Long Short Stories/ Novellas
The Same Old Story/ The Tether of the Flesh/ Golden Rain/ Grief/
The Swap/ Boredom, Or, the Yellow Trousers/ Mary's Visit/ The Kelpie from Rhum

Travel and Ethnology
The Hostile Sun
Summons to Ruwenzori
Peoples of the Earth (20 volumes, deviser and supervisory editor)
Tribe, The Hidden History of the Mountains of the Moon

Biography
Thomas Brassey, The Greatest Railway Builder in the World

Current Affairs
Today's World (Editor)
The Book of the World (deviser and supervisor)
Immigration and Enoch Powell

For Children
The First Dog to be Somebody's Best Friend

Screenplay
Deadline

A Prefatory Comment

by A N Wilson

This is a beautiful book.

The Dante scholar lost in a dark wood, the Bishop going into the darkness where God is. The man who has experienced love on so many levels, reliving his past before confronting the great Empyrean.

This impressive narration isn't just a stream of consciousness. It is well-crafted narration, it has a plot. Marigold is very vivid, but the other two women, Clare and Evie are also very distinct.

Tom Stacey also conveys – mysteriously – the character of the other members of the house party: whom we never meet.

Humour, humanity, passion are all here.

A Dark and Stormy Night is a superb achievement.

A Dark and Stormy Night

Tom Stacey

Medina Publishing

A Dark and Stormy Night

Published by
Medina Publishing Ltd
310 Ewell Road
Surbiton
Surrey KT6 7AL
medinapublishing.com

Design & Layout: Catherine Perks
Cover: Taslima Begum

ISBN 978-1-911487-25-8

Printed and bound by Opolgraf S.A. Poland.

Tom Stacey asserts his moral right to be identified as the author of this book.

CIP Data: A catalogue record for this book is available at the British Library.

Explanatory Preamble

The driven mind of Simon Chance, narrator, carries certain abbreviations and possibly obscure terms which occur on the page as they do in his thoughts. These include a scatter of Oxford University abbreviations: LMH for Lady Margaret Hall and BNC for Brasenose College; PPE for Politics, Philosophy and Economics; and OUDS for Oxford University Drama Society.

The abbreviation CMS stands for Church Mission Society. BCB liturgy refers to (Cranmer's) Book of Common Prayer.

He is caught up by the mystical thinking of the Dominican Meister Eckhart (c.1260–1327), contemporary of Dante Alighieri, of whom he is a devoted scholar. In a theological context is the Greek term *eremia* meaning a place of utter desolation, and *kenosis* – being's divestment of the 'self'.

A reference to 'Dorothy' in Chapter IV is to the (Christian) crime novelist and Dante translator Dorothy Sayers.

Quotations from the Bible spring up in the narrator's mind. Most are from the Gospels or Isaiah. Fragments of poetry come back to him. Chapter VIII begins with his recalling Henry Vaughan.
Later in chapter VIII Simon's mind invokes Jesus' injunction to the busy-bee Martha, *unum est necessarium*, a phrase meaning 'only a single thing is needful'. In chapter IX two quotations from St Matthew occur, one from Isaiah, and another from the Song of Solomon.

Chapter X includes three vital lines from the apocalyptic poem of Andrew Young, *Out of the World and Back*.

Molimo, in the Bambuti (pygmy) vernacular, is the hidden shamanistic device to induce spiritual presence by eerie guttural amplification through a hole in a sanctified drum.

In the Bantu vernacular, the term *Mwamba* denotes a single member of the Baamba tribe. Their territory is Bwamba. *Wazungu* means white people, and *mzungu* is one of them.

Earlier, in Chapter III, the parable of Dives and Lazarus is haunting Simon's mind. St Luke puts the story into the mouth of Jesus in chapter 16 of his Gospel, translated in the Authorized Version thus:

'There was a certain rich man, Dives, which was clothed in purple and fine linen, and fared sumptuously every day: and there was a certain beggar named Lazarus, which was laid at his gate, full of sores and desiring to be fed with the crumbs which fell from the rich man's table: moreover the dogs came and licked his sores.

'And it came to pass that the beggar died, and was carried by the angels into Abraham's bosom: the rich man also died, and was buried; and in hell he lifted up his eyes, being in torment, and seeth Abraham afar off, and Lazarus in his bosom.

'And he cried and said, Father Abraham, have mercy on me, and send Lazarus, that he may dip the tip of his finger in water, and cool my tongue; for I am tormented in this flame.

'But Abraham said, Son, remember that thou in thy lifetime receivedst thy good things, and likewise Lazarus evil things; but now he is comforted, and thou art tormented. And besides all this, between us and you there is a great gulf fixed; so that they who would pass from hence to you cannot; neither can they pass to us, that would come from thence.'

for

Henry Maas
a man of letters

'A l'alta fantasia qui mancò possa;
Ma già volgeva il mio disio e 'l velle
Si come rota ch'igualmente è mossa
L'amor che move il sole e l'altre stelle –

Power failed high imagining; but as if they
were a wheel turning in perfect evenness my
desire and my will were rolled by the love
which moves the sun and other stars.'

Dante: *Paradiso*

I

Who in our besieged house party will have guessed I, Simon, was lost before I set out from the villa itself? Which of you my old mates might suspect any such thing? Not you, Hedgefund Reggie, not Charley our Chancery silk. Bullion Julian our gold buff? Fergus the merger? I think not. Conceivably, perhaps, Sir Gunther, the odd one out, who could well require of himself to see through us English in our pretences ... As for the ladies, might such a shaft of suspicion as to the state of my soul have entered our hostess Clare? – Clare, self-declared confidante in my bereavement, Clare with her offer of a distracting break in the south of France amid the 'old set' in her borrowed villa to provide the vital balm on my widowhood at last.

What can you truly know, Clare, of the state of my soul? That the very justification of my life, all spiritual and intellectual endeavour, might *require* of me to be lost – to be challenged by some such challenge as confronted Dante, in exile, banished, bereft of his inheritance; bereft of the context of his life, his coterie, his stage to play on? Shall I in my isolation commit myself to make of love whatever of love remains within me?

What – God knows! – am I doing here at all, with all these figures from my youth, if not to expose myself to my lostness, my self-deception, my sloth, my fraudulence?

Yet I didn't devise this forest-lostness. Heaven knows the havoc it will entail. Is a malign hand at work? A devil's wager with whatever speaks for God? Amid the knock-on havoc of my getting lost, none of you will condone it.

Wally, ah. Treasured Wally: the forging of your bond with me long preceded University where I bonded with most of you. *Our* bond was made in limpid childhood at eleven or twelve at school in the Grampians. You and I were the risk-takers. You and I dared. Secretly, recklessly. You are here with the rest of us in the south of France only through your Violetta being a sixth-form college crony of Clare: that slender chance ...

Might you have guessed, Wally, that I was *seeking* to be lost? Inviting kidnap by this forest under the assault of unanswerable questions, *Why am I here? What am I doing in the uplands behind St Tropez, with a bunch of past comrades among whom I am little less than phoney* ... bereft of grief at his own bereavement of the wife who gave him her very being, bore his children, shaped her life to his?

No, Wally. Not you.

I am a man alone, confronted by an obligation to grieve he cannot fulfil. I gaze upon a space vacated by another of whose soul I am designated custodian. What absurdity is this? Who has the custodianship of another's soul? ... Marigold is a hollow, a vacancy, a skull a man picks up, turns in his hand, peers into the sockets of the eyes and has him questioning, *Who might this have contained?* What soul implied has flit? What monumental significance? What partner of its Maker? What the creative imperative that won the justification for the myriad of genes and impulses that this cavity contained? Its claim on immortality?

O skull, O Marigold. Five weeks in earth. An echo-chamber, long rehearsed at becoming *nothing*, dementia-scoured. A vessel of extrusion. O Marigold of the declaration *If I did not have you I would not want to live. I would not be alive.* Yours is not a hollow I can overlook.

How shall it be re-occupied by all you were? Music; memory; all, indeed, of myself that you'd dare receive … with whom I had preserved the thread of devotional exchange to the final moments of life.

My grief's rehearsal dragged on and on. When the curtain rose, nothing was on stage. When we buried you, we buried rags of history, scraps of composition, musical wisps. O skull. How do I mourn you? At your funeral we were going through a programme of motions. We the quick were cremating a simulacrum, a dolly.

Only you, Wally, will think no less of me at finding myself singled out, stripped to the buff and bolted into the pillory – to all others an object of worthlessness and fatuity whose private parts and white skin and pat existence are to be done with – just another human body, albeit breathing. Its white skin (they may come to notice) is imprinted with countless words which are already fading in this Mediterranean exposure, and warped and stretched into illegibility. Simon Chance, Bishop.

Wait, wait! Among the bystanders at the foot of pillory shall be Evie. She knew the skin with her own skin and, hence, can never un-know it – knows it with her skin and lips, knows it in sleep and in the mutual loss of her and that other body's very self in the consummation of what man has no other name than love.

A man's skin renews itself every few weeks, they say. Yet Marigold and I learned in Africa of the unexpected unity of epidermis and cerebral cortex. And the skin's memory cannot be expunged.

Of all this lot in the villa I am the last to get himself lost, heaven knows, in either sense. Simon Chance, suffragan Bishop, no less. A man of God, trained and salaried to have answers to these questions of eternity-and-now and death-and-life which our villa's tight company of the Recognisably Successful hadn't yet had time or occasion to delve at depth, not at least with the due diligence they would insist on for lesser investments.

If club-footed Wally stands apart, it is not because he was more spiritual than the rest of our fellows. Certainly not. Nor because the spectacular bankruptcy of his conglomerate several years ago has disqualified him from the rat-race. It's because our friendship's lines were drawn in childhood when no line is drawable between what is of the spirit and what is not. When word goes round that I've gone missing, he'll be standing to one side with that childhood look of his which says *one of us has gone too far*. It was what we uniquely shared, *going too far*.

Meanwhile, lost I am. Forest-lost.

Actual setting-out was about 4 p.m. Already it's – what? – nearly ten past six! Just fifteen hours before Evie joins the house party.

Am I genuinely getting lost right now? Of all God's footmen, me?

The shame of it. I'm emphatically the wrong person. Someone remarked this very lunchtime when I let drop my intention to walk. *Don't worry about Simon.* (It was Clare herself.) *He's a qualified explorer. Jungle-missionary.*

Just so, Clare – a quarter of a century ago. Another life, another history.

The layers of our lives, Clare, never quite let us go, do they?

Calm, then. Calm. Too early to say I'm literally lost in this *selva oscura*, gloomy wood as you, Dante, had it, straying off into your shattering excursion to become full-blown Man, virtually redeemed, by a route that took you into Hell's own depths.

You had Virgil soon to guide you, then Beatrice to inspire, spur you on to paradise.

Virgil, *wisdom*; Beatrice, *love*.

What species of vessel am I for Wisdom or for Love? I have you, Dante. And a soul uncleansed by proper grief; and a body vile, well past the half-way mark of mortal life …

Is this frenetic light-headedness of mine what you too knew of, my Dante? Unworthily. This same teasing elusiveness of any route through or back? – back to where one is recognised, the conceits and smugnesses and petty graft and grime … from where a man can set off anew and *get it right*? Or not back at all but on into deeper lostness, into more ferocious challenge, catastrophe. What inner conduct do I owe to you, my Dante?

You, poet, you *invoked* that dark wood to wrestle out the reality of your lostness. *I* am *in* the reality of this dark and lowering wood, this topographic entity, named and shunned. You will have me confront my being, in a pretty panic, in a very literal dark wood.

Selva oscura. Massif des Maures, Département du Var. Fifty kilometres east to west, thirty south to north. Massive, and Moorish. Amid ghosts of Moors on the soil of grand Europa.

I will not trace this mess-up of mine to the imminence of Evie's arrival in our midst – in *my* midst. I am imputing no sly influence invading the present with our past. A man can get lost in a forest.

Yet I haven't the least desire for it! No such impulse whatsoever, neither covert nor overt. I am not alarmed at Evie's arrival. I acknowledge no devil conspiring to have me pick a stupid track and misjudge true direction at the imminent proximity of a figure ineradicable from my being since I entered manhood. I dread the ignominy. That is all.

Calm.

Who's to say I'm yet forest-lost? Haven't I known forests? Trusted and traversed them? Haven't I read jungle tracks without a quaver of doubt?

My villa buddies, your Simon Chance has proven directional logic.

So what ails you, Bishop Simon? *Musabuli,* the pygmies named you: *He who lifts up those sinking into the swamps.*

Don't my legs work at my bidding? Do I have a moment's concern for my bodily wellbeing?

My sole anxiety in not finding my way back to the villa is at upsetting my companions in their nightly blow-out, the piggy-fest, the regular gargantuan snout-event. It's only six o'clock. There's still the better part of two hours to make it back: to turn up among them all before they've started in on frenzy … to drift in among them before they've awoken to my absence. *Oh –* there *you are, Simon! We were just beginning to wonder …*

Two hours to go before they begin to wonder, before the flickers of the frenzy.

Calm.

Yet this hour or two matters. Minutes matter. *I do not know my way back.* By eight it'll be well and truly dark.

So be it! I am not afraid of dark. At around eight that they'll all be closing in upon the salon at the approach of the conviviality obliviating the disaster of the day. Uppermost in their heads will be the latest on the global maelström, the worldwide money catastrophe spontaneously self-generating this very week.

'Your gold, Julian?'

'Price'll double by the weekend.'

'Have you been buying?'

'Of course.'

The next thing will be the obliviating – the honking and grubbery, the five-courses and duo of vintages beading the brim.

Only as they settle at the table will a voice remark, *Where's Simon?* Nine heads turn, cocked rhetorically. Simon? Simon? Each will then awake (even with a flicker of relief) at this further distraction from the collapse of the outer world by so arresting a *personal* confusion: *No one's seen Simon Chance for hours and hours. He's vanished into the dark wood* – the single one among us who's surely beyond the statutory call of making money.

Oh my dear Lord. The moment for a piercing supplication? From a paid-up subscriber?

Tell me, O light of my intellect: Who made this track I'm following just now: Beast or Man? And if man, what man, and why? Leading where, beginning where?

If beast, ought I to be following it? The sole beast surviving here is boar. I've already caught sight of his spoor, his rootlings and faeces.

If I am to follow your brutes and beasts, Creator-Lord, where will they lead me? Repeatedly there are tracks which speak of something's passage. They lead me on, but only into deeper impenetrability.

Come now, bump, directional bump! Why have you forsaken me? – you who were so dependable when I was young … in wilder, vaster, vastly darker Africa, when I was young.

How did Dante Alighieri meet it – eh, Dante, long comrade – awaking in despair to find yourself lost just like this? How you got into it you didn't know. *Neanch'io.* Dante. *Ni moi, non plus.* You pressed on, didn't you, up the side of the beautiful mountain. (Little mountains are all around me, though none beautiful, this entire massif a clutter of tumps.) At once you were thrown back. Leopard, lion and she-wolf flung you back into the density of the wood, blocking vision – back into just such obscurity and density as of these cork-oaks, pines, sweet chestnuts, *chênes verts,* mimosa, saplings. And the brambles and wrestling thickets.

This forest of mine is unremitting in every direction hectare on hectare, hour on hour. It can't be any different from the Tuscan forests of your imagination, Dante.

We get the Mistral and you some katabatic Alpine blast. A dark Mediterranean wood is a dark Mediterranean wood.

So now: I've no fear for myself, for life, for death. None whatsoever. I can endure the whole night here in the forest. A mere Mediterranean September night, a few hundred metres above the level of a balmy sea, a bit chilly in the small hours … *And anyway:* once I'm obliged to admit I *am* lost, all I've to do is to get down, get low by any descending gully and simply push on – keep pushing on wherever the lowest ground takes my feet and I can get through, by whatever further forested dell succeeds another until this dense jumble of ascents and gulches yields a cultivated valley and the first vineyards: and the presence of men, and a dwelling.

A Var *habitant* will emerge at dawn to be accosted by a solitary male stranger of indeterminate age, dishevelled, in a green shirt, rust-coloured slacks, trainers: suave, apparently English, seeking coffee, a crust and a way back somewhere.

A plausible speculation.

Calm, sir. Press on. *Calm.* You are not yet lost, not until you decide that you are. Use your head.

Up to a mere half hour ago there was directional logic to the course you chose. You had set off on housekeeper Maïté's report of a long-abandoned church she knew as a child. It was locked high in the forest on a certain summit south-west of where the villa stands, Maïté said no more than an hour or two's forest tramp-and-scramble. It was run up long ago for a community of miners digging ore out of this iron-rich massif as lately as Napoleon's wars.

Were such miners the 'Maures' who have given their name to this massif? Surely not. This fastness would have derived its name from the people of before the dawn of history, when names were young.

Maïté told she'd been taken to the forsaken chapel as a child by her papa twenty or more years ago. It was high-high, she insisted, *haute-haute*, and topped and sheltered by a craggy peak. From that open rock she had gazed upon the entire unrolling of the massif in every direction – southwards even down to the distant sea. I could see the wonder of it in her eyes these twenty years on. The church *haute-haute* had been de-consecrated oh, ages ago, and there was none to worship there now. Yet it was not yet a ruin, she insisted.

This forgotten forest sanctum had given me my objective, an imp of motive for a hike. It is what Marigold would have expected of me. I have allegiance for anything once consecrated … I demand divinity in things, the solemn universal privacy. Marigold knew.

God knows I'll not reach it now. I've tried enough ascents on this tramp and found no more than bluffs and ridges, blind with trees …

Haute-haute, Dante. To Paradiso. But you had one to guide you.

You-all, up in your villa on another top, might you come *later on tonight* to speculate after all that I was indeed lost before I started out? This carefree companion of yours from old times, the odd man in, bereaved of his lifelong companion, as the comfort patter runs; Marigold, Simon Chance's eccentric choice, mother of twins, lady of musical gifts abstruse and rare whom virtually none of you got to know – knew only *of* – whose music you never heard a bar of. 'Remote', you classed her; *standoffish* you thought in private if you thought at all as you scurried on with your own lives. How odd of Simon. You, Clare, were never reconciled to my having married Marigold. The Simon Chance you knew wasn't the Simon Chance who chose Marigold to wed – Marigold the reserved, driven, demoned, self-caged … whom only I knew how to uncage and then but rarely. And then she was gone to mindlessness.

Am I not correct, Clare? In my masque as lover, swain, you had me cast quite otherwise. You had me cast swaining your nearest soulmate at Oxford University.

Yet even you, Clare, stopping to think, must see that however stark her contrast with Evie, my violinist Marigold and I found love, *lived* that love – in better in worse, leaning one on another, quelling pain, easing strain, assuaging sorrow, kindling courage, kindling music. Cleaving year upon year to banish darkness in a dark continent, she with her fiddle, I with my history of abstruse astonishing redemption, aspiring to a life of the spirit, of faith and works, saving lives, praising the gift of life. Oh we saved many a life, Clare, saved fever-bellied totos, victims of kwashiorkor, faraway. Mine was no parish priesthood in Northamptonshire.

Now that Marigold's gone from me and from this world, might you now be quick to link this forest-lostness to the final, final loss of the helpmeet who oh so capriciously made her life with me?

You would still be on the wrong track. It was not life's candle going out that bereaved me of the wife you never got to know. Bereavement stole in years ago, a silent intruder; a presence in the next room, hooded, uninvited. Thereafter, Grief haunted the home. Marigold's actual death was less a death than exorcism, when the rag-doll that had been Marigold had ceased to twitch and the hooded familiar had vanished. I need to grieve, I wish to grieve. I am deprived of the ability to grieve.

You can't know, friends, how a man responds to his wife in the husk, to the joke usurper of her who was once bursting grain, spurting music. He would love the husk as grain on behalf of his God who loves all that He has made and unmade. He *postulates* love, a love they knew, and finds it there while the demon reels her back into infancy. He humours her with babba-talk, distracts her with baubles, jollities. He brings on the clowns. He makes the house a dolls' house. He shapes for himself an inanity to mirror hers. He is a man being widowed by stealth, bit by bit as her own synapses of recognition, memory, grasp, are stealthily coated …

Is that *other* any longer present? Has Love any purchase? May a man love the human space Love once occupied?

This was she he vowed to love for better, for worse. Year upon year vacancy leached the substance of her being. *There, there.* Sweet bond of love. Month on month the railing desperation – *I don't know who I am.* At five in the morning: *I don't know who you are* – from within her solid glass enclosure, unshatterable, impenetrable, a nightmare wideawake, at five in the morning.

Lord, look upon this your child that has been dragged back out of self-command into the terrors of infancy.

Wait.

Out of this infancy there self-spins a thread of infantile trust which is exclusively ours. Such pristine trust is yet of *life*, yet of *joy*. In fleeting indestructibility such a thread outspans space and overrides time. It is a moment's thread of sheer melody as of a violin which he alone can draw forth, yet a thread self-spun no less of him than her.

Such infant trust is of an innocence that is pre-dementia and pre-guilt. In these silken moments she has a beauty to which his eye alone can attest. No matter how long the preceding passage of madness, how cruel the waters of oblivion, here is melody spontaneously released, the eyes kindling and a hand pushing forth as if into nothingness yet finding … *his!*

All will be well, and all manner of thing will be well and innocent after all.

What did you know of any of this, old friends, as word reached you of Marigold Chance's insanity? Which of you paused?

By sheer slackness of imagination even the best of friends have strength to bear one another's misfortunes. I've held nothing against you Clare, let alone Wally and Violetta, that not one of you chose to call on me as Marigold's vacuity took up residence. You knew, but you chose to stay away. My mediaeval Oxford hideout was unexposed, hiding what it had to hide. By that same slack token it will have occurred to none that what affects me now is no recent grief but an *inability to grieve.*

None of you was at hand to hear the silence at the end of that interminable emptying of being when the breathing stopped; not one of you at hand to hear *that* silence. There was none there across the room to regard the survivor with his incapacity for grief as he gaped beside a heave in the bed; beside the thing waiting to be boxed and made ashes of.

I didn't expect it; no blame, old friends. No complaint. We don't do death these days. Just a box, a vibro-organ and a disposal: a little industry little spoken of, with a long face in the job description. The afterlife went out with the waltz. Don't pause, chums, to consider what that interminable closure had left sitting there in a metal chair on the linoleum in silence under the power-saving light: the interminable terminated.

Which of you could know of such protracted inability to reach across the abyss and slake a crazed isolation with two drops of recognition?

This is I, your husband, lifelong, for-better-for-worse, your children's seed-sower, investor of your body with a meaning.

Good Ambrose begged to put Marigold on his prayer-litany of the sick at Trinity's evensong, *Marigold Chance,* among that miscellany of our Oxford acquaintances with known affliction. I held him back because this was one of ineluctability, whose alleviation was its own advance. I framed my motives for declining Ambrose's offer. While she still had capacity to express a want, it was to die. The only honest petition in the throat of the prayer was *to die.* Shall that be our eucharistic entreaty, Ambrose, in your ecclesial throat?

Let it be God's decision, Simon. It is for us to pray.

None of you has seen, none of you has known. Evie alone will have perceived something, darkly, through her own dark glass in me – perceived how guilt might lie amid the elusive grief …

Get a move on, now. Standing here vacillating won't get you out of this.

Marigold, genitrix of our little line; carapaced, riven, conduit of inspiration from the other world of music, where are you? – you who went on loving me *despite*. Does soul keep you reassembled and in peace passing all understanding? *Requiescas.* May you rest, my gold Mari, in the ever-living rest of how it might have been. There's music to reunite us, and the joyful expectancy of music now that you have a hold on your evanescent being by release from creaturehood. Amid the music of spheres, your shattered fiddle's restored. One who was my Dante's contemporary, that Meister, reveals the *no-thing which transcends the created being of the soul, not in contact with created things,* this no-thing sharing the nature of discerning deity. How it is *one in itself and has naught in common with any thing.*

The Meister's words are here in my head. By his bleaker Northern route he tracks the soul to that further Presence, *a strange and desert place, rather name-less than possessed of a name, more un-known than known*: the negation of negation. You would have me pre-bereaved, Meister Eckhart, beyond grief because beyond creaturehood where the very authority of the givenness of love is in its transcendence. So you required of us, Meister. So it was you told us *we should live in a way that the whole of our life is love.*

Yet to whom shall this love be expressed? And how, how? We are but creatures, Meister. Fleshed humans. Conceived in flesh. What would you have of us in bereavement, in guilt? Were they right after all to arraign you for heresy, Meister; for requiring too much of us in the name of that God which is nameless, *nichtgott*, non-God; *nichtgeist*, non-Spirit; *nichtpersone,* non-Person?

We have not reached you, Meister … your level.

God knows. Not yet. We cannot find Him by the glassy sea, in one perpetual light, one equal music.

Only now, in our godless age, might we re-approach you who outflanked us centuries ago. You found the soul of man, Meister, this soul we are, in the embrace of the Creator prior to His *ebullitio,* His bubbling-forth demiurge, conjuring soul, beauty, music.

Oh Mari-mine, is such a place your allocation? And I to seek you there, where the beauty here in earth will have been transcended by what is otherwise eternal?

God forbid. In that music is here, it is because it was always here, in this earth.

As the affliction stalked you and the demon took possession, you would cling to me as if to existence itself. You were that child of Schubert's mounted behind his father at full gallop through night forest, *mein Vater, mein Vater*. How you would blurt to me in your shards of clarity that you *no longer recognised yourself*, that you *knew you were not the same person you once were*.

Can you now see me, Marigold, scrambling through this night-threatened forest in flight from my own emptiness?

'I cannot *compose* … I have the skills, there's nothing there.' The fingertips accustomed to make your music now clamp the temples. 'Nothing. I am so regretful.' Such a tidy word. 'All I want to do is die.' Fingertips disorder your hair.

My fingertips take your wrists like culprits, to take them into custody.

'I have wanted to die for months.'

An hour earlier I would have had you in a capsule of oblivion, even laughing. For you, every moment is always. Hence *now*, tears in paroxysms.

Your practice had been to stride the banks and eyots of the Isis on your own, generating music in your head, jotting down a phrase or a chord or a rhythmic pattern in your strapped notebook.

'There's nothing I can do with all my skills. My ideas go nowhere.' You cling to me.

'You have me,' I comfort. 'We have each other … And all those compositions ready for countless performances. For ever and always, darling.' I make some old clowning antic.

'It'll pass,' you say, meaning the creative impasse.

It will not. It will not.

And *then* I mourn you, those measureless months and years: they will pass, as everything passes, the parade of vanished opportunities, truth by the glimpse … My riven Marigold, for whom I am trustee of your gifts – gifts of God's inherent music, his spheres made personal in you, for you, by you.

I will marry this man, you said, *since he honours music.* We met in music. *He is a man of honour, a man of what he calls God; I will be wife to him, helpmeet, whatever he seeks to undertake, in sickness and in health; for better, for worse. As this manual saith.*

The vessel is broken at the wheel and the shards scattered.

II

Present Lord, I am halted on this track. And where on earth is this track taking me – the track of my feet and my recent recall?

Not to any abandoned church's recorded vista of a twenty-year-old childish memory. This corner of wood looks unfamiliar and alien.

Setting Sun, you are scarcely discernible through the foliage. You are hiding within an eerie sky that's been thickening and swelling since morning…

The density of the atmosphere bears on me. I sense the weight of it.

Vaunted bump, my old interior sextant, Simon Chance's very Ariel! Have I taken you for granted too long and you have quit my service? Which way have I been moving in this past hour? East or west, north or south?

Even if I were to know, on what compass bearing would I now adjust my route?

Use your head, Simon Chance. Stop, think.

I have set off approximately southwards, seaward in the generality, intending to return within two hours by a broad self-navigating circle … The treacher circle has slipped its noose.

So now, I am to pick up clues to the route I have come by – the confluent and dividing boar-runs, that glade made by an umbrella pine, that dark waterless gully, that forest-buried man-abandoned breccia.

Surely these half-recollected clues are recoverable to guide me back.

North, therefore, declare yourself! The sun's obscured by atmosphere gone fuzzy and its light already failing. What hope of vantage point in this tree-smothered maze of ravines, clefts, ascents and cwms … unless I chance upon my original objective: that pinnacle Maïté as a child had looked out from above the abandoned church?

Marigold, Marigold, you were present loss, there and not there in our midst, day upon day, month upon month, year upon year. Crumbling, fragmenting. Flaking.

'Is it true we were in Africa?'

'Yes, my darling. Fifteen years.'

'Why?'

'We were doing good. Bringing light. You brought your music. I brought the God of Love. We each taught them. To sing and praise.'

'I had a son.'

I respond with an embrace, head tilted against yours. Eyes were no longer configured to meet.

'I had a son,' you have repeated.

'You know we did, my darling.'

'Jasper. Why did he die?'

'It was meningitis, darling. You remember, how at Fort Portal … '

'Samueli said it was the evil eye.'

'You remember Samueli! But it was meningitis that took Jasper from us. In an infant there is so little anyone can do.'

'Samueli said it was the Evil Eye. Africa's Evil Eye.'

'We cannot believe in witchcraft. We cannot allow ourselves to.'

'Samueli was one of your first converts.'

'He hadn't fully shed his old beliefs.'

'He said it was the pygmies' revenge for your going among them. And something I did wrong.'

'You know quite well it was nothing but meningitis. My pygmies sought no vengeance, had nothing to avenge. Let's not go over it.'

I clutch you: you pull away.

'I just want to go home.'

You are for ever packing and re-packing to *go home*. To tell you we *are* at home only serves to rile you. This lost inner home of yours is never locatable. A uterine home, a foetal home. 'One day soon,' I have learned to respond.

There is no call to pack for the womb.

'Is it true my parents are dead?'

'I fear so, darling. Thirty and twenty years ago respectively – your Dad and your Mama. You forget. We all forget.'

'Nobody told me. I have never belonged here. Ever since I have been here I have felt so ill.'

The dread litany.

Daemons had *always* circled you, your familiar Eumenides always kept you in their gyre. They were circling even when you and I clung man-and-wife in shared endeavour and intent, in the foothills of Ruwenzori and in the equatorial forest. As I let in the light of God's love and you were at work 'doing the humanity thing', your demons circled.

Give love and love will do its work. This was my precept. God knows it's in me still.

You could never forgive Africa for Jasper's going. To you it was always the *sacrifice* of Jasper to Africa – to my very vocation in Africa. Like Isaac's sacrifice, but un-aborted, no entangled ram is substituting my boy. So went our firstborn, our only son. The twins were never compensation, were they? – paired girls conceived unwittingly by grief.

What is cannot compete with what *might have been*. You resented the twins' arrival for breaking in on your mourning. When, soon, you were serenading them with your inventive fiddle, the serenades were half-lament. I do not know if the quality of love is deepened by lamentation or clouded, or both of those. I caught my breath. In the forest they were to listen to your fiddle round-eyed, agape, half-circling you in wonder at the inwardness evocable from all men's depths and flowering as melody.

For all this I could not but love you. Yet such a gift of music had its own dark double which swung you out of the light of your creative gift, out of levity and hope into depths where none could reach you. The gift and its black hole. Your Janus-genius was to conduct you by pathological descent into dementia. Entering there, my old love, stunned by fog, how you scurried in panic to my side! – to cling to whatever remained recognisable to you in me. So began my own bereavement, in the days before any coherence of your fragments was gone and nothing remained but fragments, in a void defined by one woman's ability to munch, evacuate, and breathe.

Hark me now, Marigold, who've left me bereaved of grief. I invoke you as flit spirit. Dante Alighieri and I devise our beliefs like artists. Cross back, Marigold, out of purgatory or paradise or hell, cross back to hear me, how religion is our loftiest *art*, how we leap dimensions, populate infinity with finitude, making finitude holy, *whole-ly.* You did it with your fiddle, Marigold, improvising to our twins and Bantu villagers and supremely to our primal fellows in the primary forest of ancestral heritage. I fill my conjured heaven with the Company of Angels like the birds of Oxfordshire and Gloucestershire (*would that there were birds here, just a few spared by the Var peasantry, by each season of massacre*). You remember, Marigold, how I was an Angel at our first encounter, one of Newman's angelicals in the chorus of Gerontius' *Dream* and you minstrelling among the second fiddles in the Royal College band.

'People don't die like that,' you comment, meaning Old Man Gerontius.

'How do you know?'

'It's Christian make-believe,' you retort, putting down your teacup. There is a 20-minute break in our rehearsal, at Holy Trinity, along the road from the Royal College.

'*This is the best of me*, Elgar wrote on the score.'

'The score's marvellous,' you concede.

'Well then, let's let go into it.'

'I do, don't worry. But nobody dies that way - *compos mentis*, faculties intact, all stations go for some other world. We don't buy it, Simon. These days.' From behind the pure exquisite forehead and the freckles peeps the atheistical socialist. You had been watching your father go, at 59, racked and disarranged, in terrible protest. Christians are to blame for being alone in not having to deny death. It irritates you.

'If I seem to go along with your Christianity it's for the music.'

'For the music it inspires,' I propose.

'Inspires … provokes … '

We had properly met only the previous week and, though attracted, wary. Willing nothing, I had seen in you a woman of unconscious allure scarcely awake to her body. A perversity drew you to me; the incongruity of a Christian toff with his own sense of musical adventure. Your response is aggression masking timidity.

'Not,' I put it to you, 'for the deeper music they both draw upon? *Both* the holy gospel *and* Elgar's or Pergolesi's urge to compose at all cost?'

My church choir's sopranos and altos are doing Pergolesi's *Stabat Mater* next, you among them.

I have pulled you up because you aren't sure whether the 'deeper music' has validity in the Marxist rotes you've been reared in. Behind the freckles and an awaiting mouth you are in panicky alternation between defiance and deference. An iconic public school and Oxford are enough to stir rooted resentment. For my part, musical gifts like yours in one so feminine make me catch my breath. In these few days of acquaintance, you've not held tight to what your Dad would require of you, which is to class me as a spoilt Fauntleroy cushioned by a theistic credo long outdated. You've been snared by a gravitas in me. Now you're questioning my question about the *deeper music*, and weighing up a notion as implausible as a *coupled* origin for a will to make music and a will to worship God.

'Music and divinity go arm in arm,' I follow.

'There's no indication Jesus was musical.'

'Contrary Mary.'

' – gold,' you append, opening your eyes. They penetrate, those eyes. This is our first real encounter. 'What made you a parson?'

'I'm a curate, not parson. An inferior species.'

'A parson in embryo … '

'To hatch in Africa.'

'Really? So you've taken the pledge. Or should I say, *plunge.*' Boldness bucking the shyness.

'Plunge,' I confirm.

'Why?' – with eyes challenging.

'I had a summons.'

'Just like that. Voices … '

I am half-mocked.

'Can a self-respecting woman sing the *Stabat Mater* believing nothing?'

'I can sing a poignant story. Pergolesi believed; that's hard to doubt. But he was dying.'

'So if one's dying one is liable to delusion? And what about the monk who wrote the words … '

You make a *moue*.

'It seems a peculiarly tenacious poignant story,' I suggest.

'And peculiarly improbable.'

'It makes for faith.' I let a little silence speak. 'Like dying Pergolesi's.'

At the Royal College up the road, intending to compose, you are effortlessly versatile, yet pull against the dissonance and serialism they have you students venerate if you're to be performed.

Now the dark eyes gimlet me, with calculated pity for this Christ-obeisant son of privilege. Yet I perceive a plea for recognition. You have fallen for me. In a moment's loneliness the plea has caught my heart.

'What is there for you Christians to tell out, Simon Chance?'

You begin to list them. Praise and thanksgiving and adoration. Sorrow and contrition. Serenity and comfort. Ah – entreaty. Four modes and moods.

You have numbered them on your fingers. 'The actual words scarcely matter. It can be done almost as well in vocalise. I grant you there are Masses which are masterpieces. But of music, not dogma. If there's a *Dies irae*, as a rule it's theatrical bombast.'

Faith, I remind, and you frown. 'The compositions wouldn't otherwise have happened.'

'Not invariably. Janacek. Brahms … Agnostics.'

'Gripped by the same relentless conundrum of Being. *Being* confronted by its opposite.' You narrow at me. 'Nullity,' I add, 'confronted no less by Brahms or Janacek than Bach or Pergolesi.'

You have softened into attentiveness.

At the Proms up the road we were soon to hear, first, Bruckner's Third Symphony: I come out in stunned certainty of the transcendental majesty in all creation – as do you too. Next night we hear Berlioz's *Te Deum* with a choir of 400 and the mighty organ and vast orchestra: you emerge more convinced than ever that Man has made up the whole religious thing.

Then one evening we are just down the road in my church on

Prince Consort Road. I have you by myself in that exaggerated space, with its soaring windows and all the aristocracy of heaven flamboyant on a gilded reredos in full relief behind the altar. We are so small and momentary, I in my cassock with a Eucharist to conduct in ninety minutes and you in gingham but of blue like a gingham virgin. The church's silence in the heart of the metropolis is overwhelming. You've let yourself love me despite yourself: *that* I recognise – despite what you've been brought up to suppose, that ours is the post-Christian era, religion irredeemably discredited, a fomenter of wars, disseminator of obscurantism, opium of the people. Obedience, Chastity, Poverty! Absurd injunctions for a modern-day unshackled socialist. For you to love such a thing as me is yet another dialectical fragment due for miraculous synthesis …

The church waits in utter silence, we two negligible parcels of live warmth side-by-side in the front row of fixed seats below the marble chancel.

At length I murmur, 'Faith is encountered in the desert.'

You quote your *recitative*: '*A voice crying in the wilderness* … '

'John is meeting the silence … and listening again. Elijah, Isaiah, Ezekiel, John.'

I let our own silence speak. Are you gazing up at the figure dead centre tortured on its cross … or frowning at it?

'At the crux of that cross,' I tell you, 'there is *nothing*. That's the significance of the cross. That crux is nullity.'

'Nullity, Simon.' The word becomes echo.

'The still point of the turning world. But there's a body on it which moments before was alive and in appalling pain. Now nothing. In a little while it will be alive again. The world will have changed.'

I come back out of our silence. 'We people of Christianity work our own paradox. It is an even grander dialectic than that of Doctor Marx and Herr Engels.'

'There's a joker in your pack.'

'Eternity, yes. Now and eternity. The fundamental polarities without dimension. All or Nothing. Having nothing, possessing All. We oscillate between the polarities. Jesus is our synthesis of a kind. He gives Now the substance of Eternity.'

'The missing quark,' you contribute.

'Jesus is an historical figure. But his substance lives on as Love which itself has no substance. Marx didn't deal in Love. Love plays no part in his ideology, in what he put value on, set store by. I would put it to you that none of the things men and women and children and you and I truly value has any part to play in the Marxist dialectic.'

'Love, you say … '

'Love, and art, and worship. Loving. Creating. Praising and praying. What else do we live for in the context of our existence? Love, art and worship, merging, interchanging. You compose, I praise.'

Your eyes are fixed on the altar screen and its laden cross. I persist as gently as I know how. 'They're all economically meaningless, those three. A good Marxist will reduce Love to the reproductive imperative and the primal requirement to protect the young for the survival of the species, Music and Art to some pleasure principle – the entertainment industry. Worship is of course an opiate. Was it a pleasure principle that had Beethoven in all but total deafness wresting from himself his last quartets?'

'Beethoven was compelled to keep on composing.'

'Precisely. *Compelled.* So are you. What compels you?'

At Holy Trinity with our sublime acoustic we are soon to perform the *Missa Solemnis*, late Beethoven. I sense alarm in you. You want to answer but the question has you cornered. It is I who venture: 'If I were to allow myself to love you, Marigold, it would be because you in your music are probing for the truth. Are inwardly *compelled* to. That's what all art is about: probing for the truth. And all worship likewise. Letting self go into this truth. Losing the self. Think back to that Bruckner,' I say. 'You were lost in it.'

Your silence is affirmatory.

So I follow, 'We are never so much ourselves as when we lose ourselves.'

My adage came to me in the sublimity of another's arms those few years earlier. Since then I had only touched such self-loss in my vocation for the priesthood. Self-loss in God. Yet the *discovery* of that truth had been by the flesh: I acknowledge as much even at that moment. In another's bed, at Oxford.

'Losing oneself ... ' you echo.

'That is the treasure. The paradoxical pearl. Of great price.'

We stay in silence.

'In worship,' I venture, 'in music, in any art ... '

'In love,' you say. You have already confessed to loving me.

'So I also think. These three.'

'They are linked, then.'

'For sure. But the custodian is always the creator, whether or not acknowledged. Janacek considered himself a non-believer. All right. Yet his most inspired work was a Mass.'

The alarm in you has flit. Into the ensuing *quies* enters a recognition one of another without boundaries: ... as in the exposition of fine music a long-expectant rest precedes recapitulation of all that has been opened up so far.

At length you ask: 'Am I to love you in that custodianship? Like Janacek's?'

You tilt a sandy head against the arm that has slipped round you. We are flagrant in that front pew in my lordly edifice, each of us with Martha tasks to be doing, the cassocked chaste seducer and his liberated virgin.

You sharply raise your head. I can tell what's coming: 'You can't expect me to have faith in the divinity of Jesus.'

'The word "divine" isn't in your vocabulary, is it? In your music it's unspoken.'

'I'm not sure what you mean, Simon.'

'The sense of wonder – that's divine. Your music has it.'

'Wonder,' you whisper.

'Which releases the spirit. What Christians call the Holy Spirit, it engages the *whole*. The spirit is movement that flits or swirls or scuttles between the polarities. And simultaneously, presence of Christlikeness.'

'Are you talking sense?' How hard and harsh.

How harsh. 'Don't blame words for their limitations.'

'What do you mean, engage the polarities?'

'Reconcile.' Then a better word. 'Marry,' I say. 'Life and death. Nothing and all. Now and eternity.'

'The still point,' you give me back.

How you yourself do swing.

'The still point of our turning world. Crux of the illimitable figure-of-eight' – I trace it in the air – 'pivoted at the non-existent ego-point between the conscious and the unconscious. Both immeasurable open loops, the spirit at the gateway. As at Pentecost.'

'And they spoke in tongues.'

'As reported. You and I are talking prose. Peter and his friends at Pentecost had broken into poetry. In Luke's record of Peter's address to the assembled crowd were no fewer than six quotations from the Torah, all passages of poetry – the Psalms and Joel and Nehemiah and Samuel. The sheer sound of the recollected poetry was inspiring them. They were infused with how the inherited texts were authenticating their own astonishing news of the death and resurrection and what that must mean for mankind. They had been so long *pent* with what seemed inexpressible. Now they were *literally* inspired, and all those listeners from Cappadocia to Ethiopia who'd have had some acquaintance with the Semitic language group and its rhythms and inferences and colourations, picked up the meaning of what they were hearing. Some supposed they were drunk. Certainly they were drunk with their own exhilaration at what they had discovered, like those drunk with love. They had discovered indeed eternity in the now, all in the nothing, sanctity in the profanity of human love. They'd let go and were flying. Like a composer in full flood – Schubert, Wagner … that *is* the Holy Spirit, who spake by the prophets and the poets and the composers. Like you.'

I have silenced you. You have heard me. Silence overwhelms us.

'With your fiddle,' I dare to add, 'you straddle the dimensions. You do let go into the truth, Marigold, the fiddle under your chin. What true human being can do otherwise? It's the proper human condition. We don't have a choice. We can contrive to duck it until we come to die. If we've left it that late, we know we've missed the point of the gift of life.'

'Faith.'

It is a murmur. You are gazing at that reredos, its elemental images, as if to accuse it. I have no sooner caught you than I lose you.

'It's the *natural* condition, Marigold. The motive of hope in the *conscious being,* the only durable motive. The human race, the conscious being. Why do we rejoice when a baby is born?'

'Faith in … '

'Love. Faith in love equals hope.' I have stumbled on the dictum. 'Love is your quark. Person-love. Divine love. The same word serves: it cannot but serve both. What Jesus does for Christians is to personify love. We meet Jesus in the desert where hope is not discernible.'

'You said.'

'The desert of nullity. Pointlessness. Which Silenus insisted was the logical state of mind.'

'Silenus?' And I tell you: Dionysus' minder, speaking of Man as Mammon, only Mammon. And you follow half in mockery: 'Your Jesus points the way … '

'Jesus *is* the way. He becomes the way for us, through discipline, through our submission, our acts of veneration. You already have the discipline in music. Quiet discipline. You too have the corpus of musical inheritance. I might call that the communion of saints – the whole inventory of musical discovery, musical wisdom. You perform at a high endeavour.

'Jesus applied the Tao-term about himself – *I am* The Way. He gives it being. He responds to our situation of mortality amid the All. He lived a life in time amid the timeless universe. He allows us to be *of* it all in its entirety.'

'What do you mean *allows*. We are of it whether we recognise it or not. Why bother with it?'

You shock me. 'Listen,' I say. 'You compose and perform. I preach and praise. It is the same requirement, the same impulsion from the centre of our being. I would say, of *being*, that very being which is the gift of all humanity.

'By dint of consciousness we have to square that reality of participation in time and in eternity, in space and infinity. We *must* do this … by love, by art, by worship – in whatever combination of the abandonment of self. We need that truth, that wisdom, to live within, to belong to, to give expression to.

'So Beethoven writes his last quartets out of deafness. So John of the Cross his erotic poems as God's ravaged lover. There is that famous adage of a twelfth-century monk of how the love of truth, *that* truth, drives him out of the world, and the truth of the love draws him back into it. That is the sublime oscillation. My love of truth calls me to the Ituri forest.'

And I begin to tell you how in a few parts of the world there persist communities which are uniquely symbiotic with the natural world around them as if symbiotic with the universe – communities living wholly within and upon their own Eden: the last of the hunter-gatherers … Chukchis and Inuits in the Arctic, tribes in Amazonia, in Papua, Bushmen in the Kalahari; the remnants of uncontaminated pygmy groups in the forests of equatorial Africa, each in their way of life and patterns of belief our ancestors of an Eden-innocence.

'Before paradise was lost.' Your intervention comes with condescension. 'I hardly suppose you're a creationist.'

'It's myth, the creation story, intended as myth, to tell a truth about the obligations of human attainment of consciousness, grasping the *I* and its equivalence of *you*.

'A beast dying for its young is not saying *I* and *you*. It and its young are a single organism driven by instinct. A man making conscious choices has gone beyond instinct. He chooses this course or that course. The right one or the wrong one. Good or evil. Wise or wild. Rational – you'll go for that – or irrational.

'The intention of the myth of Eden is to place Man in the same ground as the Creator, where he cannot but belong, yet Man with his weakness and selfishness which consciousness obliges him to be aware of.'

'Your pygmies, Simon, won't be pre-Fall any more than the rest of us. They'll have eaten your Eden apple. They'll know about blame and guilt and fear of death. And if I'm wrong, they won't need you.'

I hear the briskness in your voice, an intolerance of cant.

My response is inadequate: 'They cannot but be closer to Eden ... '

' ... which means wholly preoccupied by the requirement to survive ... '

' ... with whatever savagery that may entail. Yes.'

'Pre-conscious savagery. Therefore, innocent.'

'They are not savage in the familiar sense. No gratuitous savagery. They're shy and gentle. What we do in slaughterhouses would appal them. I don't doubt we sophisticates have something vital to learn from them. They're almost extinct.'

'Yet you're intending to Christianise them.'

'Proper Christianity squares the Conscious with Innocence.'

'Proper Christianity!' It comes as a great sigh as if *proper Christianity* were ever possible.

You would love me loyally in the teeth of my conviction and my fantasy. My Bambuti were indeed pre-Fall. No one had told them they were naked. If anyway they were children, they could not *become* 'as children'. They hunted, they gathered; they lived, they procreated; they died. They had no space for good here and evil there. They had space only for what was there for survival. 'Proper Christianity' would not even save them as a community in their primality. Those proclaiming the divinity of Christ would bring them booze and clothes and prostitution, debt-slavery and AIDS. You and I had more to delve in them – their proper dark – than ever they might learn from my churched faith, run by their Bantu quasi-masters.

I would delve the very bulbs of the innocence that Eve and her consort had lived before they knew that they were naked and warranted redemption.

You loved me post-primal more than you intended, Marigold. More than you bargained for when I put it to you that you might join me as partner in my response to my 'vocation' of which the very word brought on a half-smile. Because you learned, as we all learn, that love is not conditional and not eradicable. It is not to be bargained for. It is not amenable to planning.

You made me your true-love for the sheer perversity of the choice. In the social cosmos of your fellows Simon Chance had to be a toff, a genetic throwback, programmed as a Christian. You summoned the humanist and the egalitarian in yourself to match what I claimed as faith. Yet that love took root, and grew with its own delineation, for better for worse. Be it in the service of Bantu villagers at diocesan headquarters or of hunters and gatherers in the forest, *I* would preach my Jesus and *you* would offer music. Each of us would bring the written word. Somehow we each would ease the lot of equatorial Africa's post-colonial needy, you in guilt at the imperial heritage, I in virtual honour of it. You were restive for challenge. Playing in the back row of the strings in a provincial orchestra and cajoling your friends into performing to tiny audiences what you composed was not after all to be your route to fulfilment. You were to take a risk.

Your Dad, you said, would have approved that risk. The way you put it was that he would have condoned your marrying a public schoolboy and Oxonian from what was left of the landed gentry for the chance of making him 'recognisably human'. You were paraphrasing his imaginary response in jest, and kept loyal to both loves, him and me.

As memory leached from you, I was the last companion of your vanished life. In St Saviour's you knew not where you were, nor who you were, yet it was I you still infallibly knew, as a recipient of your love, and provider of your grub of being amid the mush of oblivion. The currant eyes (now wild) for a moment see me as I am. A hand darts towards me like a prayer spurting.

Love once given and received is indestructible: that I've learnt.

'My Dad came yesterday,' you tell me. It was three weeks before the end. 'We had a beautiful talk' – he who surely loved you too, Lecturer in Sociology at the University of Keele, gone from this world in flagrant suffering these 30-odd years, whom I'd never known but for the heady erudition that framed you.

A beautiful talk, I echo. My hand is squeezed.

In echoed love your Dad encounters me, he who had no time for God, no time at all. In the manner of *your* going, you made mockery of the Gerontian way of dying as did he.

III

O you friends of mine up there in the Villa Les Maures, taking showers, splashing cologne, getting kitted up to re-assemble and re-review the debris of your expectations, be warned. Be warned. Within the hour you'll be awakening to an absentee from the midst of you, a special one, of statutory detachment edged with purple, a make-weight for the golden calf (now visibly melting), one whose student values, such as they ever were, were surely no different from yours. Pause now, regard: you still have no hunch as to his incapacity to shape the bereavement to which your hostess alerted you. Meanwhile, he has disappeared into your adjacent wilderness.

The other night in his dream your old friend – would you believe this? – was on a precipice lip, the sharp edge of the Great Gulf Fixed as depicted in scripture separating Abraham in Heaven and Dives in Hell. Indeed, I was wearing Dives' mantle of episcopal purple, and there in Hell with all my fellow dons at Trinity, a gaggle grown fat and lazy and of irredeemable, complicit self-satisfaction. Just how wildly was I imploring the patriarch in heaven to send me Lazarus – ex-beggar, covered in sores, ragged at my gate. Yet Lazarus was also hunched in my living-room and was Marigold in disguise. So then it was *Marigold* in heaven, across the Great Gulf Fixed! It was she pleading to *dip her finger in water* and *reach across* the terrible void to cool my tongue: the tip – just the tip of her finger!

Lazarus-Marigold had become a child of sheerest innocence.

Oh but the gulf was too wide! The abyss too terrible! Communication unthinkable.

When I awoke in disorder, the same unspannable chasm had become my guilt. I dream, I had gazed across at you, mouthing silently, but nothing now was capable of passing between us, not an exchange of eye, let alone the touch of a finger. I was now the one locked into a slab of greenish glass, peering through it to you. The ruthless tableaux of dreams had transposed the scenario of your nightmare.

Look, Jesus, look on me in pity, how I – purpled-up – sumptuously fare, here now in the Villa Les Maures just as at High Table at Trinity year by long year. Each evening I'd flee across the road to College Hall from my pledged spouse's flaking into non-being. Did I not long to sweep up those flakes and shards and bin them? *No, no, no*, I admit no such longing. You breathed, you spoke, you smiled, the button eyes ranged our living room to fix me in imbecilic *trust*.

It was for me to enter my own kenosis divesting *being* of *self*, to provide you a twinned presence in a willed void.

How is Marigold? stopping me in the Broad, in vacuous solicitude. I reply,

The condition advances.

Sounding cold, I add, *She had a good day yesterday* (not groaning aloud to be gone, not pleading to go home, not railing at inability to make her own music).

It's wonderful what you do, Simon.

Do? Wonderful?

Classic FM plays for you at table in the kitchen. There was recorded music seeping into your own room, to lull … lull-music to rise up and accuse you for playing no part. You demand it silenced.

Of course you've thought of St Saviour's, they persist in the Broad. *Though it is expensive.*

I have thought of St Saviour's, and more beside, Charis, Beverley, Willa, my pavement comforters, speculating what I have done to earn this. I am to have you put down? – consigned to a half-way grave, a bin of flakes and shards of what once were people? A costly elegant bin, another mini-industry of obliviation?

When in the end I *do* consign you, my halfprayer is misshapen. *Lord, furnish me with a vessel of recollection of this life-long helpmeet,*

maker of music,

mother of our daughters and of a son sacrificed to the tropics.

When the ambulance crew came to the flat across from Trinity to carry you down the stairs you had not descended for months I saw in your eyes a different quality from their blankness. They said,

treachery.

Oh … O God, behind that accusation, enfolding it, was beseeching *Love* such as rose, itself, out of fathomless depth in piteous defiance of her own extinction.

You had only weeks to remain in this world. As if I didn't know it would be thus. You died of accelerated emptiness.

The darkening of this forest of the Massif des Maures is accelerating. The recollection of you which elbows out all the rest is the treachery.

In those months which became years before I consigned you, I in my library down the corridor from you would be alert not for your call or whimper but for the carer's key in the lock. It would be half past six, the start of the vigil, the washing, the feeding, the nightly masque of Encarnacion's bustling cheer. You weren't fooled. The images jumped and slid silently on the television screen. The fingers at the hem of the comfort blanket once so brilliant were a clutch of bones. You never spoke Encarnacion's name, never quite knew who she was except as harbinger of the escape of me, the spouse, the vow-maker.

I escaped to Hall, grief mangled dry of tears, prayers of intercession husked. In Hall I can turn quite riotous. Trenchering, quaffing, imagination on the high wire, I am Dives in purple and raw-skinned Lazarus in oscillation. My fellow dons long ceased their *How's Marigold? ...* – except for that evening when I arrive in Hall with my skull plastered. I tell them how you had smashed your violin down onto me like an executioner. I made light of it. The Furies, I tell them. They furrow incomprehension. Your Mittenwald has been the treasure of your life since you inherited it at twelve, the artificer of your craft, symbol of your creative gift, your *fétishe* which my God, you hissed at me, had made off with. 'My' God was your masked enemy until the doctor changed the prescription secretly administered by Encarnacion and we doped you out of conjured demons.

That evening, I let on to none of my co-dons that it was after I had rescued the violin from the open fire in the grate that you seized it from my hands to make it a weapon, screaming *I want you dead.* Nor how I had fled bleeding into the bathroom to lock myself in until Encarnacion arrived. I emerged, still clutching the remnants of the violin. I could hear in my head the wonder of the sounds you had once drawn from that depths-of-the-forest instrument, the improvised evocations; inward, exploratory, ecstatic; most secret of yearnings and flashes of joy. My heart in that bathroom was as broken as the wood and guts in my hand. I could have silenced my colleagues into dumbness by the scale of your tragedy. That sacred instrument had come to be the single and supreme link with your fellow men. What you could draw from that violin and what you could improvise for it had become justification for your presence on earth. What that very instrument summoned in you was what had seemed to reconcile my returning with you to this Oxford of mine when I opted Trinity's offer a lectureship in mediaeval Italian: Oxford so alive with music that you would surely find an *ensemble* to join and perform what you had composed.

That was the way I put it, when I knew there was something other for me than the role of a West Country suffragan bishop of my inconsequential self-destructing Church, which I loved and wept for in ragged pity. My flock was scarcely flock but a gaggle of souls with clerical vows and functions riven by issues of esoteric concern to paid priest, as to the gender of those in high office and the sexual practice of certain incumbents. On neither issue did the gospel of the Son of God have bearing, nor on the relentless matter of the dispensation of diocesan cash and property which cluttered my desk and consumed my energies. Consider the lilies of the field, how they toil not, nor do they spin. I was not a bad suffragan bishop, striving but blunted, exploiting gifts neither spiritual nor scholarly. You perceived this, Marigold – my privy irrelevance, my hollow office, after no more than half a dozen years of endeavour, when Trinity's offer of reprieve was slipped in front of me: their looming vacancy for a Lectureship in mediaeval Italian literature. My *Triple Essay* had quickened my collegiates' awareness of my sustained engagement, my lifelong armature, when the book was greeted with strange gratitude by a literary establishment taken to rooted secularity.

I was touched, and the scholar in me was tempted by the space and grace to do research and write in the name of my Faith upon a specific Christian enlightenment in a given place at a given time, and its towering exponent, while the intellectual verve was still within me.

Yet you, my Marigold: for you I sensed Oxford spelled danger. Oxford was your spouse's prior citadel of privilege, his sealed inheritance, whose codes he knew and argot was conversant with. Once she had remarked *You're a different person, Simon, with your Oxford set.* 'They belong to a generation ago, my darling. The set.' The old gang, Fergie, Reggie, Julian; Clare … *Evie.* 'I will be at work on Dante the metaphysician, and supervising eager young things seeking new truth in ancient wisdom. Meanwhile, Oxford is full of music … ancient and daring.'

'Yes,' you said. 'Daring.' And we embraced.

Yet within two terms of our moving to Trinity there appear the maggots, the grubs of your oblivion. Lapses of musical recall ambush you, your fingers jumble your intentions. Gremlins jostle your musical imagination. You are incredulous. When the diagnosis comes you are already beyond grasping quite what it must come to mean.

Ah Marigold. By then I am half in prayer for the *hastening-on* of obfuscation. Direst of all are the splinters of clarity. *Then* you rail, my ambushed darling; in such wild despair you turn to me. 'Things drop off,' I repeat inanely. 'We grow older. Things drop off.' (You are not out of your fifties.) 'You are surrounded by love.' Whatever of *you* that remains to be surrounded.

Then I pray for your oblivion.

When you declare to friends that you are still composing, you believe it. I catch their eyes to share an object of pity – *you* …

Ambrose's glance thrown to me across the table in Hall implies something Christian is to be garnered from it all.

What, Ambrose? That mischief which wheedles substance into non-being and time into shards, and what-might-have-been into a wraith of love?

This is no Oxford that I ever knew before.

My forest track has led me nowhere.

There were you, my Marigold, in 'real life', capriciously reachable, will-o'-the-wisp, in mute inchoate plea. Blown memory snuffing one by one the candles of recognition of those you were bound to, who embodied you, components of your person. Out went the trembling flame of each of your children, and there was I alone in semblant recognition, I your love, sower of your body …

   Late into the morning you lie there on your bed. You have half-dressed, and then seemingly returned to bed. Your hair is brushed. Your eyes are closed and your mouth is turned down. Can I detect any rise and fall of the bedclothes, telling of breathing? Might you be without life? Such a possibility has me looking beyond your apparent lifelessness, the down-turned mouth (do people die in bed with mouths turned down? Or is a sign of disgruntlement a sign of life?) – looking through you, my spouse, to myself, to my own response to the possibility of you being gone – your being without *being* any more … in that now, if dead you are, this spouse, all is at last too late; the opportunity to love is blown, the whole redemptive thing for the birds. Somewhere I have failed you, and as you have shrunk away from me into infancy and diminished from spouse to patient to wraith, so what stands in for love is rote. I bend to kiss the motionless mask. It jerks aggressively aside. *Go away!* it cries, and knows it has dismissed me, me and my rote, more or less for ever.

   For what I have learned at that moment is that it is *too late*. Too late.

   Can a man pray retrospectively? Pray to replay a scene? Might such a thing not make for redemption even now?

   The solitary candle flame that does not die is a pair of praying hands.

   How you will say (piercing my heart) when I tell you of a dear friend of past times about to visit us *Oh it's a name to me*. One by one I announce the imminent arrival: a childhood friend, classmate – your old duettist Marie-Elaine at the Royal College; our fellow medical missionary from Congo. You can recall no thread of mutual being. And when our caller arrives, indeed, your eyes surface as if from the depths of a well. A light of recognition is here, a bone-marrow gladness bereft of precision: for that hour you are younger by thirty years. When the visitor is gone, within minutes you will not know who it was that had come or if indeed any had come. The present moment has caged you anew.

Where have you gone, my Marigold, Gold Mary? You are not all there. She who would be all core is all dross. Whatever claimed to be is might-be, whatever gave shape has lost dimension. *Where? Where? Where?* Oh leaves awhirl, where is your tree? The loss of the wood of the violin of the melody is this loss.

The gifts flit one by one. After piano keyboard fingers falter (I notice, but you do not), then the fiddle fingers. Suddenly an entire piece returns to you, a chaconne learned with precision as a student, that precision counter-priming though you cannot tell me what chaconne it is nor how to summon it again, for it summoned itself. You who were never less than total in what you were and did have been selected for untotality, to be fragmented before my eyes as if an elbow had been jogged and a masterpiece of culinary art had been dropped into the scullery's sink to swirl in bits. No person any more, Marigold, but a swirl of bits. My God, my God, for what is it that I may pray?

Bits. Fragments. Fragments.

Or it was as if what once was the fabric of you, fabric of creative artifice, has been secretly invaded that I dare not unfold it lest I gasp at what the moth-mite legion has done to it. For when you would summon your creative demon and fail you are left only wishing to die, only to die. So have you yearned for 'months and months and months', by your own testament from the caged present.

Your wish has been granted, Marigold.

I pause right here in this forest to weep at my own unweeping.

Where are you, Marigold? Did I leave you desolate?

Where am I going? *Quo vado?*

Wasn't I scrambling just now a bit hectically, down by this dubious track through these interminable cork-oaks and Mediterranean pines and chestnuts?

The less sure of where I am heading, the more frenziedly I follow the vagaries of this boar-run. And half that space until darkness will fall is already gone.

IV

Let us be calm. To have taken a careless turn in a dense unpopulated forest – what sin is that? I have a life to live ...

Oh, I confess spiritual dereliction. Lazarus and Dives, the *doppelgänger* of my dream don't fit. Yet I, Simon Chance, am scholar, pastor of sorts, papa, grandpapa, I have friends, pupils, functions. I am writing a book to be read, admired and be of guidance. I have reputation and rank, which as an Anglican of breeding I don't flaunt. The purple I arrived in is an outward show of faith serving him who shows it no less than the shown. The kit props faith. Let any strangers know I don't deny you, Lord; your presence in me.

Do I not have my very own devised acronym for meeting the emergencies of all that life may throw at a man – the vowel-less CLTH?

Calm, therefore. C for Calm. Don't I know worse humiliation than distracting one's companions from their tummies and the mesmeric haemorrhaging of unrealisable wealth that served only to render them glad that they were not as other men. Welcome Calm to my heart!

Yet, Calm. You are not here within. God knows. Calm Thou art Peace and Sanctuary. I have no access. Thou art the Still Voice. I cannot summon you. I cannot override sheer shame at my idiocy, at the ravage of my imagination detailing my disgrace. This pat acronym does not fool me. Calm, you have an entrance key to your high keep, and I have lost it.

Love. L for Love. 'Bounce it off the sky, watch where it lands!' I would tell my Bambuti and they grin wild teeth at the image of Love swinging in the forest canopy until it randomly chooses to alight … My Dante writes of Love as a estate of the soul, not as any swap or wooing but a perpetual giving without any condition or selection, be it for these trees and their forest, or Death himself.

What any more do I truly know of *love*, ultimate possession that does away with self, with this crude creature, ducking, diving, concerned not so much to love as to be loved …

So T?

T for Thanksgiving, *at all times in all places.* What scripture says, it means.

At the entrance to the Death Camp, the forest-tunnel into Treblinka amid the snarling of the dogs, *give thanks.*

At Golgotha, on the Cross, in searing despair, in blinding pain, nullification – *give thanks.*

Is this what my perception of my pat truth puts me in reach of? God knows …

H, now – *my* H – for Humour, for sister Humour is to serve by ridicule to puncture all the pretentiousness of species Man, our bull-frog presumption of being formed in the image of God. We, the forked beast! Hang on to my H, and grab thereby Detachment. Elevate the absurdity of our conscious species. Make all fit for laughter? A mean refuge. My personal *Commedia* is a script for a Fool, for the wry smiles when a local headline reads *Dante Scholar Lost in Dark Wood.*

Or shall I in this particular emergency elevate my acronymic H to *Hope*? Hope is built into Destiny and invites a vowel for my consonants, a circled mouth shaping the silent *gelassenheit,* the letting-go, the melting, into

Faith.

Faith in Love equals Hope.

God, for Man, is love.

Love's essence does not alter by the measure of its letting-go-into. Heavenly, humanly, loin-love, self-abandon for thee my Lord; love's essence is one essence. Calm is but the preparation of the setting for Love.

Could I endure a week without the working of the Holy Spirit as love?

A day? A night?

This very night now closing on me?

God forbid – to be blocked or barred from recourse to hope and prayer. In this strange forest where I am alien, the fingered branches and knuckled roots alike are in perpetual collusion. I the lost man am yet the vessel of prayer. Prayer is the soul's blood. What fool says in his heart, *There is no God*?

In this crammed wildness you shall locate me, Lord. In this petty disgrace. Here, now, Lord, I could halt on this non-track, kneel on this steep hog-run, strewn with twigs and confess and *pray,* however late for the dinner-table … 'I, Simon Chance, loving Christ as Way and Truth, *hear me!*

'Jesus, who dared no definition of yourself, not even *Christ.* Jesus, who was word made flesh and, being word, not only *was* but *is* … Such self-revelation – it awed and appalled you … so that you could not but *will* your own death in the flesh, since what you were revealed as was scarcely sustainable as flesh. What are your inheritors to do now but work with every trick of beauty, music, verse, ritual, artefact, and dance to make our masque of your unworkable word? And still fall short, sinning in thought and word and deed by negligence, by weakness, by our own deliberate fault. I have left my quondam friends bewildered in their villa – my strangers-to-belief men-of-the-world who still look to me against their better judgment for succour as their vaunted substance evaporates into thin air and their fate's ground is gone. Forgive me all of you! I will have made our hostess sick with consternation. Look on her, Lord.'

Am I to kneel? Or to hurry on in the hope of repairing my foolhardiness? Any trust I had in my intended forest circuit is gone.

Enough of childish *cris de coeur*! I *could* kneel to summon up a tin god's intervention. What would my pygmies think of that? Yet when in equatoria I presumed to summon You, the Calm of my grander Christian presumption, you were counter-willing *me* tranquillity from *within* the interminability of their Congo forest itself.

This very morning, there Clare you were alone in the kitchen, chopping carrots and onions for the looming luncheon, with its guest-of-honour who, now dying, had once abandoned you.

Alone in that kitchen, Clare, you did not look up at my approach, yet knew it was I. You murmur, 'Simon, I'm having trouble with my faith.'

'Ah!'

You have confessed uniquely to *me*. However close and secular an old undergraduate friend, I am now *priest* and mystically endowed … whose *Ah!* hangs limp in the air. What you need from me is the armour of faith.

Might you not know, Clare, that Evie, joining us tomorrow, is custodian of my fraudulence?

At last you oblige yourself to pause and glance up at me from the chopping board. I am ready with my penetrating gaze: my stock-in-trade theatrical technique: concerned, rooted, humorous, a gaze invaluable to priests. Counselling others, we know how we counsel ourselves.

Yet *God* knows that if I am indeed now lost I am deservedly lost. I might more honestly have answered you with that opening stanza of the *Inferno* with troubadour Dante, *half-way through his life* waking to find himself *in a dark wood, where the right path was wholly lost and gone.* This morning I have little to give but that theatrical gaze and that weak suspended *Ah!* of ectoplasmic gravity.

Go searching for Dante's book, Clare, in Dorothy's translation, somewhat flawed, maybe, biased … yet she with a mind of muscular faithfulness that has her accompanying both duos – Dante and Virgil, then Dante and Beatrice – on the trajectory of the soul. The book's lying there open on the iron table on the patio outside my *dépendance* just forty paces from where this very morning you were doing the chopping for the dire lunch-party.

I felt sick at myself, Clare, physically nauseated, that's the truth of it, at my inadequacy in your kitchen. For lost is what I have become, in the dark wood, *selva oscura, the right path lost.* And Evie arriving tomorrow, concerning whom and me, the two of us, you will know more than I dare suppose; Evie your old confidante who will have wept in your arms because of me. Yet you this morning Clare are in full earnest in your appeal to me … It is I who keep the Faith shop, is it not? There'll be some in stock, naturally… you caught my glance of affirmation: I, Bishop Simon, acquainted with sorrow. Scoured by bereavement.

How much would you be wanting? …

Ah, so. I hear you. And what quality?

'Deny yourself … ' I propose, and on the cue you complete what lingers – *take up your cross, and follow Me.*

Such quality!

What would our chums say? They would say, 'Look, Simon, keep sensible; feet-on-the-ground. If we all went for such brand faith, top-of-the-range, how would the world go round? Your own alimony, Clare, your Family Trust, your son's success in property (doubly spectacular after his papa's profligacy), his villa here which you have borrowed for us all, your so very tastefully appointed flat in Paulton Square …

It echoes in the head. *Deny yourself.* No villas in the south of France. No tennis. No sex, no shopping. No share portfolio, no subsidizing of the Church of England's priesthood with hard-nosed investments, no spires, cathedral choirs, bolts of episcopal purple, no mission funds and Christian Aid amid the pandemics and the floods, the tsunamis, genocides and famines. It's not the world Jesus grew up in, is it, Clare? Its population has grown a hundredfold since Jesus. Fifty-fold since Francis of Assisi. Didah-didee. So what lesser line of faith, Clare, might we settle for, you and I?

Something more comfy, workable. What did you ever mean by *Faith*?

Better to come along to evensong with me in Trinity chapel for the good old BCP liturgy, harmonies uplifting, soaring and subsiding, lambent and beguiling. We'll murmur a plea for the sick, the bereaved, the mind-blown – there's always plenty to pray about. Thence to Hall, with me, mere Lecturer. Hear Grace at speed in nasal Latin to justify the roast (with trimmings), and apple charlotte (and cream), a battery of cheese. Consummating port. High Table for High Priests and their guests. Annas and Caiaphas, and their guests.

Isn't it for me to reciprocate your hospitality? It's my function, as quasi-theologian, *quondam* bishop, to fare sumptuously, be clad in purple. You know the form at Oxford, Clare, and you know I've never let go holding you in reflected affection, as Evie's confidante.

Listen, all of you up at the villa: let me blow my cover. Soon enough you'll be responding to my disappearance with exasperation. Let me tell you now: Your old friend Simon Chance, Right Reverend, is not merely no better than any of you, *he is grotesquely worse.* Amid the panoply of his cloth, his rank, his calling, recognise him as *fraud.*

Did he 'glory in his tribulation' over Marigold?

Was there that in him which longed to be shot of it?

Did he co-suffer Marigold's entombment? Could he bring himself to so much as dwell upon it and *give thanks.* At all times in all places? Here was suffering the imagination would not make space for. Which of you my friends has heard the sound of weeping that none is meant to hear; so solitary, so desperate, so loveless, weeping in a chamber – a *cave* – of such infinite darkness that its walls retreat as they are approached? It is a cry which the crier knows cannot be responded to whether on earth or in heaven, and yet a voice *I* heard – *and near I yede /in great dolour complaining tho:/ 'See, dear soul, my sidès bleed,/quia amore langueo.'*

Ah, Marigold, long pard, the other warmth in the bed – my ears and heart did catch that throat's despair in the long months that followed diagnosis. What novelist could dream up such torment? By its own definition such amnesia is not imaginable amid the clutter of our faculties. A cry trapped by and in the pit of pits.

My old dutchie, companion-in-life, to whom and in whom vows bound me. When in my arms, rocking, and there came forth from you the repeated plea *I long to die,* I was not to pray that you should live.

The reeling back of your being into infantilism and tantrums was not any source of charm.

The discovery of what life might have been is made when life is being dragged away.

Listen, friends, *this* old student friend of yours (classmate, team-mate, messmate, mischief-mate) when you went into the City, the Law, Politics, the Civil Service, the running of your inherited estates, into all busyness of business, eccentrically proceeded quite elsewhere. He responded to a *calling* no less, astonished at himself. He heard a voice *Whom shall I send?* 'Send me.' He spoke of it as a 'post-imperial' vocation with the adjective intended to forestall the chaff about the white man's burden. The soul sought those who had never heard of Jesus: to whom the primality of this Jesus might be unfolded amid the primality of those submersed in their natural world.

Simon to the Pygmies?

How puzzled you must have fleetingly been. *A calling.* As if there was that authority to issue any such calling! *Whom shall I send?* – send to carry innocence to the innocent … to define innocence on innocent soil, enshrine childhood for children and by enshrining save childhood's elimination.

The days of the white-skinned missionary were history. Already for at least a generation it was 'our' Bantu faithful bringing the gospel to fellow Bantu. They warranted the fervour. The Jesus-god would blind the Evil Eye with love. But who would reach to hunters-and-gatherers clinging on in the intimacy and darkness of the forests, a lesser species of creation in the eye of any Bantu Christian? It would be left to one eccentric whitey, *mzungu,* scarcely known by Africa, to engage in such an endeavour. *Send me,* craving a prior innocence, craving their nearness to Eden where the knowledge of good and evil was still locked in a thousand species of plant and grub and creature. Send him who craved a rooting and a rootling for his own faith and function in the pristine world bequeathed to man by God, and craved the resurrection of his sister's love-child, lifeless in his own hands.

The very circularity of my intended forest route would restore me to the abandoned forest church – if I were not already lost.

Regard, my friends, the superannuated prelate, widowed don, prayer-spent, wound out, pushing sixty and destitute of joy. Of course, I'm different from the generality of you. But different in any way that matters like Julian our bullion buff? The rest of you, these past five days since my arrival among you, you've been watching mesmerised the value of all that allows you to be what you suppose yourselves to be *dissolve*. Your portfolios of investments, hedge funds, your real estate – all haemorrhaging by double-digit percentage points each passing forty-eight hours. A week or two more of this and you'll be as destitute as I – yet I out-destituting all since I postulate another order of value. I bank Truth.

When we were young, there was Simon Chance, one of the lads, a fellow rough-and-tumbler, quick-witted, idle, mischievous no less at Oxford than at the big school, game for whatever's going – had I not an ear cocked for something inner? A singular voice?

It surprised you all.

Except perhaps you, Wally. For you and me there's the *childhood* anamnesis to share from when we were eleven or twelve. You were spared the scourge of football because of your foot and I assigned to be your fellow rambler. You were with me when I found that ptarmigan chick, unfledged, yards from the snowline and exiled from its ground-nest on the bald bleak heights overlooking the Ericht gorge which was out of bounds. We nursed it secretly on milk and pellets of bread. We made its nest in the pile of sack-race sacks in the sports kit store at Talladh-a-bheithe. We loved every fragment of that bird, we watched its down become feathers. Then it flew. Such was our inexpressible joy that Highland May! Something within each of us learned that very day to fly... A twelve-year-old at chapel at our prep school, Wally – you tone deaf, I a solo chorister: had you not already scented my other world? Did we not share it? You and I would swap our dreams, sorties of imagination.

In that Grampian wilderness of Rannoch I surely told you of the delectable vale that lit my secret imaginary life, my specific vision of this world transcended. From my high point of jumbled bens, *there*, suddenly far far below, light-drenched, a vale I knew to be of ultimate peace and bliss, a site of soul against the bank of a vast river of crystal water which curved away into a limitless distance, the site of soul on its exquisite shore lying some three or four miles ahead of where I stood and two thousand feet beneath me from the elevation of my high col. Beside the sheen of water I could make out with acute precision yellow rocks and verdancy. Arduous traversing of a wild tract of peak-studded uplands had brought me to this sight of beckoning paradise. There could have been no other route than that I'd chanced upon. I knew the astounding privilege of the sight being vouchsafed to me. This was the sacred destination of my being, stretching infinitely below me. And *my* being was also *all* being. To descend to it awaited some point in my future, an apotheosis to come – a descent by a confusion of clefts and rock-strewn cwms. Yet I hadn't any doubt I would reach the place when it was to be ordained that I should.

Surely you'll remember my speaking to you of this waking vision, Wally? In our gabled Highland bedroom on a summer's night with the sun scarcely troubling to set? As children we took each other as we found ourselves. Life was full of discovery – our own: our comrades'. And of all comrades you were the last to be puzzled, years later, by a *vocation* having caught me up.

Vocation wasn't a word either of us would accord much meaning as, after Rannoch, we grew into manhood by our diverging routes. You were to learn of the family business, buying and selling, money-changing, margins, profits, losses. Several years on you heard at a distance of the ordination of your childhood friend: you were not non-plussed. You were momentarily reflective of how otherly indeed can be two prep-school best friends – and preciously *other* as to the directions life would later carry them. You might have glimpsed a line of insurance against your world's exposure as ultimately futile … Do you remember running into me once at Heathrow airport at the height of your spectacular entrepreneurial ascent? I was returning on leave from my dark Congo, and there were you in the baggage hall. You ribbed me *For God's sake, Simon, when are you going to settle down to a proper job?* One of your enterprises was cultivating tea in western Uganda, not far from my mountains and my forest pygmies: *I can't help myself, Wally*, I answer you; and you stop to look at me, sweetly incredulous. Yet you are soon to crash, and when you did you could not help yourself.

As for the rest of you with whom life was shared at public school or university or both, breaking in on maturity – oh yes, I have discerned these decades later a curious strain of gratitude. One of your own, Simon Chance, whom you'd known in the blood as you were taking shape – here was the self-same fellow investing not in the gilded pit but some quite other fairy ring of Weddings, Christenings, Funerals, Thought-for-the-Day, and Christmas Carols to welcome the birth of One to be judicially murdered for the threat of his truth … who would return mysteriously to life to trump mortality. You've all picked up the puzzling mythology.

I am woven into the backcloth of your growing up. This arras you can't discard. We are all in our weaves together. We've all knelt in chapel, all heard Grace intoned, invoking *thankfulness* for *life*. Yet what your chum Simon Chance's subsequent vows expect of him would be scarcely comprehensible to any one of you … except (at moments) Clare; Clare confidante of Evie.

So up at the villa I am the pale custodian of the hedge against your world of supposed reality being exposed as unreal. One of you, our arriviste Sir Gunther, distinguished, rich, *déraciné*, Zurich-born, must suppose himself immune from any need of a pale custodian. Because Gunther Brunner has arrived, readymade a grandee of his adopted England, who has taken Clare's chum Pauline, lately of St Hugh's, an aristocrat's daughter, to replace the first wife he grew too English for. His Englishness is of a higher carat than we ourselves would dare to claim and is enough of a sphere of being in itself.

Not one of you has an inkling of the daily orisons I maintain in secret in my *dépendance*; how in the lower garden by the tennis court I pray. How my vows endure. That which the darkness cannot comprehend endures. Once it reflected joy, that same joy Dante came to know and kept him writing, kept Dante on his progress on to Paradise by the hand of Beatrice. I don't disown my Credo nor jettison the chance of escaping this dark wood.

You old friends are variously on the gilded treadmill in the golden pit, generating wealth for the noble sake of generating wealth. Children of God, you have nodded to him at the weddings, christenings, funerals and the rest, furrowing kindly at the unworkability of what it proposes. *Those who want to save their life will lose it, and those who lose their life for my sake will find it.* Whatever next! What next? Can any such injunction sustain a civilisation? A market? A bourse? Next week's provisions for the family table? *We believe in One God, maker of money*, which paid for our fees to attend the ancient seats of learning where these comradeships of ours were so worked that all these years later we're still woven into the same arras.

Your religious life, Simon Chance, is the luxury extra. Be reminded. Yours is the costly ointment from its alabaster jar smeared on the head of your Jesus as his murderers close around him. Judas had a point, grousing that the money would be better spent on the hungry. These past few days, our *real* world has been in demoniac descent onto the Gadarene rocks. We foregather at our drinking hours and sumptuous meals heady with disbelief …

Today our very special guests were late. Could it be that they had hit the rocks and died?

We were assembled in our villa above the forest for our pre-prandial obliviators. Our *Telegraph* had been brought up by Maïté's husband from Cogolin, nestled sleepily below among its vineyards. The newspaper was instantly dismembered. With taut courtesy each in turn – Fergus the merger, bullion Julian, hedgefund Reggie – snatched apologetically for sheets of newsprint any one of which would be carrying its own take on the scenario of finality … Page one. Leader column. Business Section. Interpretative article by the current economic high priest. Each column of print assuaged the ravening for doom for a few brief moments. Even Sir Gunther himself, secured and index-linked, sneaked a glimpse, though he'd rather it was the *Guardian* whose heart bleeds visibly. Wally alone, busted by the last big crisis, held aloof with nothing much to lose.

Oh, *impatience* for Armageddon! When war is declared the suicide rate plummets. Yet another bank is to be snuffed by the twist of events – can it be the Brothers Silberberg, stanchion of the universe? Nothing is sacred; none shall go unshriven. The C of E's pension fund is but another House of Cards. Our cathedrals will stay upright in their decay, staring out as from Easter Island for God knows what.

O sackcloth, O ashes.

As for me, in the face of this version of death I am not so much afraid as terminologically intrigued. I too could be swept away – my Church, my rank, my scholastic role ...

We await our guests.

Fergus, you of such brave aims, I overhear you ringing to annul your flotation on the London Stock Exchange of the Chinese consortium you have so assiduously constructed. With such grace do you let the whole thing go! In a matter of hours, indeed of minutes, the earth beneath has moved and rendered pointless the shaping imagination and unrelenting endeavour of months and months. You have encountered a Will that nullifies all for mice and men, and by that Will's ancillary grace you submit.

You were never one to bother God, Fergie, doing your PPE at BNC. Yet here's this grace in you, a spring of saving grace. The whole thing – the city's manifold endeavour – is a game, a monstrous *charade*. Let the merger go. Ta-ra.

Let the world unravel. Let each day's fragment of history be overcome by the next's ... Don't we see, Fergie, Reggie, Julian, Charley, how events are devoured by history and its media as if by locusts? Nothing survives but stubs and stalks. The locusts swarm in, darkening the sky. Tomorrow, today's news shall be yesterday's misfortune, and yesterday's news is nothing but where the locusts were.

Friends, it is you and you that fill the headlines and crave the column inches, you the bankers, investors, legal eagles, citizens of distinction, of authority, bulwarked and bucklered. The news has swept upon you and devoured *your* husbandry, your portfolios, discretionary trusts, endowments and safe havens; your reputations, elevations, laurels of honour. O Ozymandias.

O Almanac de Gotha, O Directory of Directors, the High Priests, fat cats and Sadducees. Friends, sub-friends, chance comrades, merger Fergie, bullion Julian, Chancery Charley, hedger Reggie, old pal Wally (who has foresuffered), Sir Gunther Brunner – dare you look to me for some other motive for your endeavour upon earth than getting on top and staying ahead of the game, the money game, the status game? Dante declared the mountain of Purgatory held *e nulla pena* no other pain more bitter *ha piu amara*, than for a life of avarice. *You shall not love the world or the things in the world,* John told us all in words which will not go away. Dare I repeat it for you? Dare I gaze back to you as it might be ancient John clinging to the threads of his life, dictating his last brief letter to the 'children' of his fading heart and whisper on to you that truth?

Would that I could dare.

I have not retreated into the desert for my restitution, to any cavemouth, to cup my solitude and silence in empty hands beneath a juniper. I'm in the pots and pleasures of the rich, the cord of the habit frayed, cord of the one-time missionary of Jesus who'd trek through the Ituri rainforest to bring God's word of love to bark-clad innocents in a doomed endeavour.

This superannuated suffragan bishop of the C of E, scholar of Dante, recently widowed, has lost his way in the forested massif of Var, some miles west of Cogolin, to the dismay of his hosts and ridicule of the natives. No such man can come back to his fellows and show them a further reality.

V

L ook how the big hand of my watch is already at the vertical! The hour is seven and nightfall imminent.

Take stock, fool. Here's a track long unused yet seasons ago roughly opened out for a 4 by 4 vehicle. No one's ever stripped the cork-bark from these oaks: it's too deep in the forest. If peasantry from surrounding valleys made such a trail it would have been only for their boar-hunt when they surge forth in mid-winter to massacre every furred or feathered thing of innocence and beauty in celebration of their humanity. Else it's to serve fire-fighters if the forest catches fire as I have heard it devastatingly can.

Physically to escape this forest is a doddle. Can I not follow this very track's route to some superior track and so on, *out*? Yet it at once disappears in undergrowth. So then, all I have to do is stick to any *descent* where rainfall flows *when* it flows and so escape the maze. But it'll be late into the night and leave me heaven knows how distant from the villa. And the forest of my lostness will have followed me.

Man of God, creature of idiocy.

At the first dwelling I chance on, I'll knock up the wide-eyed *habitants*.

'Vous êtes d'où?'

'C'est une maison qui s'appelle villa Les Maures.'

'Villa Les Maures?' A rough brow furrows.

'Au fond de la forêt. Au sommet d'un colline.'

'Vraiment?' Bronzed puzzlement. *'Je ne connais pas.'*

'C'est vingt minutes en voiture de la petite ville de Cogolin.'

'Ah. Et vous voudrez la téléphoner?'

'Je ne connais pas le numéro.'

'Rien de numéro?' No number at all? Residual sympathy evaporates.

'Rien de rien.'

'Et le nom du propriétaire?'

The blundering Englishman in his green shirt confesses in broken French he hasn't the least notion as to what name his hostess' son has the property registered for any listing of phone numbers. Quite likely a nominal company protects Colin's incognito.

The peasant grape-growers will give me a corner to doss down for whatever is left of the night. In their own good time they'll ferry me to Cogolin. At the *gendarmerie* they call off the alarm and deliver me with a French shrug to the Villa Les Maures and present Clare with a bill for the aborted search. For within a few hours the alarm will have gone forth, police alerted. *'Un de nos invités est perdu dans la forêt. Un homme.'*

'Quel age?'

'Moyen. Un peu gris. Pas trop ancien.'

'Il s'appelle?'

'Chance. Comme chance.*'*

'Et ce monsieur Chance: comment il s'habille?'

'Une chemise verte, nous croyons.'

The system rallies. The more it rallies, the vaster my ignominy, the more voluble the apologies from my house party after their ruined dinner and dreadful night, when I'm dumped back.

Meanwhile, at 9 a.m., someone will have met Evie and her booming Victor at Marseilles airport ... *Simon has disappeared.*

In the lost hours I shall have shrunk from heroic victim of unknown misfortune to laughing-stock. And Evie? What might she suppose? That her approach pitched me into mindless flight?

Are we negatable, Evie, by caprice, by folly– *you and I?* Yet it was you who in your e-mail at the approach of this encounter whispered the word *panic*, and I who brushed it aside.

Listen, Evie, listen. If I am to be briefly lost, such a mischance befalls anyone, any time. A deceptive fork in the forest track, a clouding of the sun. Yes, yes: I ought to have been carrying a compass, a phone, a number in my head. That was a little absent-minded – no worse than absent – sauntering off in green shirt and cotton slacks, one-and-a-half euros in one pocket and glasses in the other.

So what option have I but to follow this track down, keep on till far into the night and walk out somewhere? Maybe thirty minutes of daylight remain to me and another ten until absolute darkness. What track will then be discernible? There'll be no moon with this queer high murk, no comfort of a fleeting, feminine moon. Chaste moon is banished.

Yet in this last light I could still retrace at speed the virtually trackless route I have come by and pick up a directional clue. I might still intercept the by-road that links the villa with Cogolin. Surely I have a chance of making it back to the villa by midnight. ...

Be smart. Be lucky. In full darkness it'll be impossible ... and if I fail I'll have delayed by several hours my emergence from the forest by means of the first alternative ...

Here I hesitate on the steep descent scarred by immemorial deluges. It is silent and airless. Not a dark leaf of these brooding cork-oaks quivers. This entire forest is expectant. It is in league with an imminent future.

As for this scurrying, fretting body of mine, the stuff of its inhabitant is to be put to the test. I shall have it retrace its steps with its lifted toe-nail even if the last part of any such circuit will be in pitch dark. If that fails, *Dante Scholar Lost in Dark Wood* is the awaited headline.

But they won't be chuckling into their apéritifs up at the villa. A ruined dinner is a ruined dinner. There will be no leading on of the Fool to have us rise above it all.

My feet with lifted toe-nail shall indeed attempt retracing their steps so far. Hurry now, hurry.

I shan't succeed. I am to be assigned to this forest. This crisis is destined. This cup will not pass from me. This forest is my destined nemesis. Regard these trees before they disappear in blackness. See the aisles they make, cathedral precincts, sanctums, sanctuaries. Here I am to be lost, to find myself if such is to be granted. Here choices must be made, here only inner light will replace the encroaching dark. I am *half-way through the story of my life*, like Dante. Six centuries ago life was shorter. Today drooling middle-age hangs on to its middleness so as to shroud finalities. My fellow ecclesiastics and I wrap ourselves around in roles and reputations, our Africa committees, with scholarly conclaves, coteries of College, freemasonries of this sort or that, each with its rituals, some with their vestments. They comfort, they cushion, they obfusc, easing the passage of one day to the next. What comforts us most surely is our own voice sounding sagacity.

Brute destiny has conjured this forest to call the bluff. Here hides an old barbarity, a destiny impervious to love, to the gospel Christ, his invocable peace, the context of thanksgiving. Here bides Evil awaiting its sway, indifferent to any plea of man, deaf to blandishments, the pomp and the pretension of the creature Man. In my bones I know well it is decided already that I shall not recover the route I came by, that I am to be captive here, that these aisles and cloisters are to vanish under shroud of dark, under another rule that has caught me up to play with me as it will. In my old rainforest when my little companions go hunting colobus monkeys in the tree canopy, they shoot their arrows and yelp their cries – *wah! Eriah!* – to separate a single monkey from the troupe. Once isolated, they know they have him, and pursue and torment him in his lonely terror until he makes and misses a dramatic leap. Then they have him, as this forest's Evil now has me.

Oh my villa friends, how we suppose we play the world, deluded in the troupe, we who between us know how to turn a profit in a falling market, who will never be quite outsmarted since even when there is nothing else we have with us this man of God, one of us, Simon, to take the last trick; our broker-boy, the ultimate hedge. With this conceit, dear friends, this chutzpah, we have woken from half-sleep in his pit that Evil of sullen destiny. We have provoked him to do what he will to the monkey-man who got himself separated from the troupe on his primal forested ground, to take possession of him and make play with him, his blood and his body in its green sports shirt.

For you comrades up in the villa it's now crisis and, as the *Telegraph*'s Business Section headlined today, you're *staring into the abyss*. So too am I. Your Abyss was surely always there, yet only now do you find yourselves staring into it. Such is *your* brute destiny; I've left you to it, regrettably unavailable to provide salvation of a different order, my old ex-juvenile fellows of the ruling caste, the prospective great and good, suited and barbered, under layers of self-preservation, ranks, trusts, pensions index-linked, health insurance and share-options, titles and honorifics, gracious and grace-and-favour residences, intellectual slants and shibboleths, rote moralities, simonies and tax evasions, marriages and infidelities, divorces, separations, vaunted conjugal endurances; your fortunes, follies, vanities, rebuffs; sagged foreskins, withered dugs and squandered lusts; pilasters of the community, patrons of art, aficionados of the concert hall; *arrivistes* and aristocrats, bankers, brokers, wheelers, dealers, lords and landowners, Fergus, Julian, Reggie, Charley, ruined and rescued Wally and the unsinkable Sir Gunther, each spoused or re-spoused with his Henrietta, Jane, Philly, Pauline, Violetta, June … and hostess Clare, divorcee of distinction, paired for this occasion by a one-off bereaved ecclesiastic, scholar-bishop, a spiritual lush engaged upon the *nth* penetration of Dante Alighieri's parable of infatuation.

May you stare into abyss, mine or yours. Mine is Hell, and its resident master the barbaric master of my destiny. He has found me out in this forest – no! he has inveigled me into this forest, lured me and misled me. It is no cathedral with naves and aisles and transepts, it is a maze and labyrinth, a vast entrapment, a catacomb of false alleys, dead ends, sumps, cloacae, not penetrable by any Grace of God, indifferent to men and wholly deaf to prayer. This is the sullen power my Bambuti knew was not assailable, but pocked and dark and masterly, biding his time to outlive love, deny salvation, stifle and snuff hope for man. My Bambuti knew him. All my life I had denied him. Now he has me.

'*Evie,*' Fergus accosted me: 'that was your popsie from LMH. Evie Scrimgeour. Scrumptious Scrimgeour. Surely …'

All today I was out of kilter. Maybe because I *am* unreadied for Evie and her consort… Something could break loose … a wild havocking joy. This morning, Clare lifted the edge of my cover when she looked up at me a priest from her carrot-chopping, for her far from ordinary lunch. The awaited guest had shaped her life by first marrying, then abandoning her. Now he was dying.

Faith isn't wrapped in packets, I put it to you, Clare. 'We ecclesiastics – ' I begin to gather myself – 'have need of our own spiritual directors, no less than anyone else. Mine is a monk named Paul … On Sunday you and I will go to Mass together in Cogolin. Half-infidels. Seeking faith, two secret Anglicans.'

'Secret?' you echo. 'With Victor and Evie?'

'Victor is never secret,' I acknowledge.

'He'll insist on church.'

You caught me on the hop, Clare. Next, you were assigning me to say Grace.

Your guest couple up from St Tropez – your Alpha bridegroom who, twenty-three years ago, walked out on you for a tall, faux-fair, ambitious girl-about-town with cheek-bones and a chic rapacity hangs on her arm as he settles at the great round table that Maïté's lusty husband's built for the very spot. From our hilltop patio the forest rolls twenty kilometres to the eternal sea.

I haven't seen your Hugo, Clare, since your marriage day. And now his crab devours him. He took you down the aisle like an aristocrat. The commanding beaky features and the noble skull to which hair clings in clumps are sharply outlined. Your supplanter, past 50, still tall, cheek-boned and long blonde, in jeans and a lace shirt with looping necklaces, is withered about the mouth and haunted. She wears the title of her exiled lord that once was Clare's due.

Succour this couple, Simon, if you are any man of God. Succour the grandson also. I have my priestly function! This Hugo will know of what I have come to profess. He could even yet be ready to receive whatever I might have to slip to the dying. At the right moment.

There was no such moment. The table-talk was typecast, wilful chaff without crack or crevice such as could be driven only by the overwhelming unmentionable.

O six-year-old mite inheritor of desiccated rank, what world awaits you and what afterworld! What will you remember of this grandpapa on lip of death? That he looks on you as justification of his having been? For all of us reared into our desiccated wisdom no more than scurry up and scurry down our barricade against the truth. How skilled we are, a scurry of sybarites, behind our barricade of verbal chaff, of drink and food, of snob-sunshine, snob sea-lane, snob snow-slopes, of cosmetic oils and garmenture, of motors, yachts, and of our very own elect referred to only by Christian name or soubriquet with whom one's been of late or intends to be with soon in this vogue rendezvous or that. When it comes to the unbreachable exclusivities of *la dolce vita*, there's strength in numbers, but not too many.

Spiritual succour, my lazy bishop?

Is this, here now, not the *point* and *purpose* of it all, under our canvas pagoda in the high sun of the azure coast, the lordly carpentry thoughtfully beflowered, the perfect little banquet, course upon course, our glasses plenished and replenished by the paid devotion of native Maïté and her kindred stream. Below our hilltop at its elevation of two or three hundred metres above the sea there rolls for mile upon mile my present forest labyrinth . . . In my Grace of a single spoken sentence I have given thanks to a Good Lord for having us live the way we extravagantly do and our having enough to lose in this banker's abyss to justify frenzy at its evaporation.

Pink blandness brushes me. O the nauseous piety of my throat. God knows, an inner voice is summoning to our feast the tutelary demons of betrayal. Sickness, fear and death infect the rattle of our chatter as we sit *gonflé* at our meat. Do I sorrow for you all or sorrow at my betrayal of you? I cannot tell. You've done right by your own lights, dug no hole to bury your talents (talents you were bred, raised and schooled for): you've worked your righteous best to dodge the taxman and fructify the endowment. Whatever comes of this crash your obituaries in the surviving journals can be pretty well guaranteed their column inches, your heirs shaped and accoutred to repeat your own fleeting access to this small planet's ranks of privilege among the species man. You've inherited an alloy of brains and savvy, got near enough to the top, hung in there and been generous *sans* risk. We've swapped the aristocracy for the meritocracy, name-change on behalf of the quick-footed. You will still have won the rubber, pocketed the stake, and held off that extra little while for lifting the edge of the carpet to sweep death under.

I sorrow for you as I sorrow for myself, guiltie of dust and sinne. Friends, we share the sorrow of the labyrinthine hill of Purgatory. But here I have my own peculiar Evil to contend with.

The inherited banking fortune of Clare's crucial guest, once so unassailable, will have slumped today with the global slump. Two wastrel offspring his present lady bore him in the flare of their romance have already depleted it. His freelance role with Christie's of London, scouting among his fellow exiles all along the azure coast for priceless works of art they might after all require to pop – products of creative inspiration honed by the artist's God-given gift that have turned into bags of money hanging on the wall: this Transubstantiation in reverse – such a role was at an end. (O thank you Lord for Music's immateriality, none's property but the soul's!)

How the grass of class withereth, its flower fadeth. The young wastrels bear the name of the bank chosen by royalty, as does their mother, while today's scion, fugitive peer, their father, is named now after an ancestral corner of the land he spurned to reside in wary exile in St Tropez. Thither he bolted from you, stunned Clare, and hence did that first son you gave him choose this spot for his Mediterranean villa – to reach toward the father he scarcely knew as he grew half-orphaned into manhood back in England. He's not here, yet he it was who devised today's meal as a terminal reconciliation between those who bore him. Your comportment, Clare, was to seal the absolution. With what style you pulled it off. This will have been Faith's last brief essay, before his coffin bears him hence.

The child, grandson, dynastic strand in long cotton trousers, is led in to glimpse and be glimpsed by him whose mediaeval honour will hang on him. He is curious and indifferent.

Dear Clare, any tranquil memory of today's lunch party (vital and mortal, meticulously staged) is to be another casualty of the post-prandial idiocy of this other guest of yours. I can already tell that the attempt to retrace my route has been as unavailing: as I feared:

nothing of my passage since my turning back has been familiar, and nothing remains of any 'north' or 'south'.

Dear Clare, everything about your marrying your find so swiftly after your coming down from Oxford was right except that nothing revealed to you whether you loved him or marvelled at him. He was *so* right, so awfully and eminently the catch your widowed mother dreamed for you, and so responsive to your breathless adoration.

Minutes after your exchanging vows at St Paul's Knightsbridge it was Reggie whose whisper pierced me as we drifted into the Berkeley:

Can it last?

All is healed up now. Oh we English are so skilled at the cosmetics of conjugal scars. To scar elegantly over such trivialities as ripped up vows and lacerations of heartbreak is an attribute of breeding. At today's table, no wounds gape. Reggie, twice divorced, sits beside Clare's looped supplanter. Our talk is of the betrayal of the England we grew up in, of which of course we are exemplars. Our conversation skirts the slump like the plague and sticks to our ex-nation's more protracted blight: its moral collapse and in particular the failure of the Church of England to rectify the soullessness of the masses …

My companions stop … the opinionated ladies, and Charley, Julian, thrice married Reggie with his pre-nup cover against another disillusionment: suddenly they are looking at me. Even Wally and Violetta. Sir Gunther in pursed detachment.

'Why is this, Simon?' say you, Clare, in mock challenge, to redeem their own lapse of awareness: this bishop in their midst, holy in his green shirt.

'You mean' – I counter – 'why the failure of the Church to convert the masses in the name of a God most of you have long given up acquaintance with?'

'Oh, come, Simon,' says a voice. It is Wally's. 'This is no time …'

'I'm rather fond of our local Anglican pastor here on the coast,' puts in his dying lordship in his patrician tones. 'He lives with his boyfriend but he'll have us address him as Father, which I consider cosy if a shade incongruous.'

'The C of E,' a spoiler bowls his googly (it is Reggie), 'wouldn't dare give us the line on buggery.'

'The Church,' I hear my voice, defending my corner, 'defends the love line, where there is true mutuality.'

'One must differentiate the orifices … '

'The hazard with the homosexual fad – '

'You think a fad?'

' – is equating any kind of erotic impulse with love. The act of love is an act of complementary self-loss. Even sacrifice.'

'Goodness me, Simon.'

Goodness me.

'So no wankers,' sums up our guest of honour.

'*Pas devant!*' Clare commands, and her supplanter glances across at her.

Eyes have scanned for the child. Neighbours tilt bottles to top up glasses, then their own. They are frowning back at me, re-cast among them on the instant into the higher order, Melchizedek's, no longer one of a rank of professionals at this or that – tinker, tailor, lawyer, gold buff, hedger, banker, entrepreneur, but *priest,* endowed from elsewhere. I hear myself remarking that Mankind loves God and God loves man as *other.* The Church is Christ's bride and he its groom as object to object, willing surrender, each for each …

My voice comes from far away. It carries no conviction. Yet you are all attending, as if indeed I might presume to be your *Meister.* 'Origen of Alexandria –' I tilt my little flask of wisdom '– by his own description, kissed and was kissed by the Lord's Word as a bride is kissed by her lover. Together they unify the otherness of gender.'

'*Vive la différence*' – it is our suffering guest again, he nearest Death, scrutinising in his glass the lees of his life. His first wife and her supplanter are impaled by a gaze of wordless dismay, our company pierced by an awesome silence.

Is it here, is it now, that I am to open for him the gate of everlasting life?

The silence roars in my head to reverberate as in a chasm. I am Peter in the courtyard, ripped of the guts to proclaim the truth which defines me.

Far below, remote and infamous, the sail-speckled bay. Around its pencilled shore the celebrated ecstasies of *Sybaris now.* There rages plague. Money-blood gouts. Buboes ooze. We have admitted this tainted fugitive, whose birthright was a bank, into our alien midst. Here the parabola of his life is closing upon its asymptote. He is not to be judged by me, neither he nor his lady: they were in pursuit of love. Yet which of us would not elect to die at home? Here is exile. What meaning has this piece of Mediterranean littoral for us English? Does he sow or reap here? Speak their language in his villa? Hold dear any crony native to the place beyond his butcher or his gardener? He was bred for another shore and an inheritance he abandoned, and on the brink of eternal newslessness hungers for gobbets of gossip about those he bid goodbye half a life ago.

I take his leave beside his Mercedes in the driveway. There he stands with his thin hand on the shoulder of his first son's six-year-old, on whose other shoulder rests the hand of Clare. This was for the photograph which Clare had staged as the concluding ritual. As for me I have failed him in my duty and my function as already I had failed his first wife in the morning, and have surely failed those others of the outgrown circle of my youth..

When I lit out on this forest walk it was half in flight.

Half-running now. There is habit here, and habitation; these tracks: a prior presence. Look – another rule is here, not knowable by me precisely yet another ordinance that is alive to my intrusion. Ruffled, perspiring, confronting what is to be deemed Evil in wilful frustration of me; him as yet unseen who has my destiny in hairy hands, impervious to love, blind to prayer, to what makes man Man; a king of his own dark kingdom in wait for one of us of soul to blunder in, to snare his human victim, mock him in his ecclesiastical conceit, this Grace-sayer. Are not his pieties fortified by his late lunch, his duck done with apple poached in honey, his chard with St Sybaris' mussels in cream, the rack of cheeses, *navarin des fruits*, and two or three or forty finest wines, the Dives-divine?

You have got me, Devil, me a rare one whose thighs are not yet withering from disuse beneath a ballooning belly. I can hear your silence in this motionless black wood, silence exaggerated into assertion that you are the master and I the intruder, at your whim and your command. *You may not, shall not, pray, Simon, bishop. There is none but I to pray to and I am blind to prayer. You have no companion in your fear and isolation as you roll in darkness down the torrent of your fate which is to be ever more hopelessly lost in this forest, my domain into which I have already led and drowned Marigold beyond redemption, beyond the reach of any supplication. This is the outrage that she knew. This horror upon you now is what she knew. There is no way out. It is your turn to submit to me.*

C'est la vie. The day thou gavest, Lord of illusion … is ending.

Each in our riviera shirts, slacks, sunhats, shades and espadrilles, the formulaic kit for the bitch-goddess, apt for the season, assembled at our villa in this massif heaped behind St Sybaris because (being that much smarter) we will, like Boccaccio's fugitives, dodge the others' plague. The Devil of these woods holds up his mirror. What chaff we are. What little mounds and curls of shit.

O mortal Catatonia, O evaporation of treasure-on-earth! O spent lives! O withered thighs! O villa in the South of France! O house in Town! O Eaton Square apartment, O place in the country with ancestral echoes, O ownership of acres, O plausible function in the

Square Mile, O seat in Parliament, O public role in the arts or, at a pinch, governance of the Church of England: enfold me as one with you.

Shaded from the high heat of the afternoon, borrowing time in a borrowed villa on its random eminence in a borrowed forest, we of vast heritage of civilisation, of elevated schooling and scholastic accolades, university degrees and ecclesiastic designations, did greet our death-fingered guest and have to offer him on his journey hence these summations of our life's attainment. Chard with mussels done in cream.

Here is an abyss to stare upon, eremia, desolation without feature, that very further void that I am trained to fill with my Faith, my Hope, my Love. Faith in Love equals Hope. Yet who is it whom the Devil now makes play with? It is I. He is my incubus. This past night in dream, he led me onto a low-ceilinged gallery, a deep horizontal fissure along the vertical rock-face above the void. I could not stand upright. The rock floor of that gallery was tilted at a steepening diagonal towards the drop into nothingness. My nightmare did allow me to squirm down to that precipitous lip … and to discover how indeed the cliff fell infinitely without projection or crack or handhold. Yet I could make out a virtually identical horizontal gallery corridor scoured out of the rock-face twenty metres beneath me, where I knew there to be trapped just such others as my self. But where I lay belly-down at that perilous edge, the least movement to squirm back up to the gallery's inner wall would have me plummeting to my extinction.

I woke in that vertiginous alarm bereft of faith in any love to equal hope. I woke in the presence of designing Evil.

Vividly I perceive Evil to be present in this forest, holding sway. It is he of a prior savagery who is guiling me, intruding his authority, precisely to impose my destiny. I am fearful of this pervasive power. The trees are in conspiracy to usurp the One to whom I made my vows and pledged my life, in whose name I pray *Thy will be done*. He's made my prayer a parrot. Listen. *Whose Will?* The will that took our son from us, Marigold and me? That will that took the child's mother from me and from her own being particle by particle?

A will of the God of Love?

Some God! Some Love!

For a fleeting episode there was Jesus asserting Love. When one of his semi-literate acolytes dubbed him Son-of-God he did not dissent. How might he know who he was? We take this non-dissenting as his assent. We had our avatar for a year or two, a goddish healer to touch, be touched by, break bread with, wonder at, hear from him stories of a superior ethic; he loving enemies, accosting his 'Father' for attention, forgiveness, protection from backsliding, from the Evil One, from Death the destroyer. Water went to wine and wine to blood and blood to life *sans* dimension.

What metaphor is this? What fantasy? What strained delusion, induced hallucination, coming back to life, inviting the finger of the doubting acolyte to probe the savage wound in the side of a body mutilated in hands and feet. The finger never did its probe. The acolyte only said, *My Lord, my God.*

Be thou my vision, O Lord of my Heart, be all else but naught to me save that thou art.

You are not here in this forest. What is here is feckless Simon Chance, with his tinsel rank in a contrived Church, in the presence of his own destiny, synonymous with Evil, of which he is afraid, on the brink of darkness in an alien forest of vast extent. He has ducked out of a phoney refuge from a world of economic implosion at a villa occupied by those of old acquaintance among whom it was his duty to stand out as a vessel of truth and fount of ultimate hope.

I'm afraid. I am alone. I am in alarm. I am no longer sure I am still up to roaming this forest through the night. A bit of a pot has crept up on me lately: I catch it in profile unawares in the bathroom mirror – belly-slack creeping up since Marigold's incarceration put paid to our Pennine hikes, tethering me to the vigil.

VI

Evie.
Evie.

Were you to be here, Evie, counter-spirit. Here in this pagan forest, to juxtapose this demiurge.

At this very moment I will be ensconced in your mind. The clothes you have packed for these few days you will just now be choosing for me to be aware of. The books you have picked will be such as to prick my interest. That unexpected novel. Some new voice in poetry. A biography that assails the unassailable or a new gloss on the medieval vision ... Berdyaev. Soloviev. What you used to call my high tarns, my spirit's comfort.

Your email read: *If I promise not to panic, it will help me not to. So I am promising!*

The answer you got was in the old style, devil-may-care, *Our promises were always kept.* Even so I took care to define our roles in the masque. *We are, as always, the best of old mates from Oxford, even dated one another under the spires, three decades ago.*

Half of a grown-up lifetime, Evie, my Evie. Before we knew better than not to cleave, one to the other. Your Victor, I daresay, is not in the practice of noticing or at any rate not noticing what might as well not be noticed. Would he ever catch the half profile of a fellow guest and see there one of devastating recognisability?

For this Victor of yours has arrived where men seek to arrive – where without you he would not have arrived. You are the jewel in his crown of papier mâché.

These next six days, that's all, all we shall have had. Six days, that's all, as overlapping guests. Six days to keep our heads, enact our minor major roles, were not the ruler of this forest to have taken me hostage.

Either of us could have dissuaded Clare from this holiday frolic. Or we could simply not have agreed to come to the villa at the same time. I left it to you, Evie, to decline … but you did not decline. All that fell to me to do was say to Clare – not write, but say on the phone – 'if Evie's game, I'm with you all at what sounds a pleasure-dome, Clare.'

'We won't have you holing up at Oxford with Dante and your gloomy Russian theologians, nursing sorrows.'

We hadn't spoken till then, Clare, in the three months since the Royal College's 'In Memoriam' for Marigold and the performance of her Threnody by her one-time fellow students you never knew. You had murmured even then of your taking over your son Colin's swish villa above St Tropez in September for a gathering of your own.

There was no telling just at that time – was there, Clare? – how Marigold's death would play out within me. As ever you were thinking of others. But you couldn't tell then where the shekinah-soul might seek its peace and light. Who indeed could tell? With what rude instinctive tact have you proceeded! When your invitation turned up on my screen you simply copied me the message you'd e-mailed to Evie and

Victor to whom you'd proposed the period of September 8 to 21, to which you'd nonchalantly appended *I'm planning to invite Simon Chance, recently widowed, from the 2nd to the 14th.*

The 'recently widowed' would be for Victor, as also the surname. Coming from you to Evie, mere 'Simon' alone would have meant no Simon but Simon Chance.

Your absence, Evie, from Marigold's obsequies didn't mean news of her death had escaped you. There had already been that note on plain writing-paper headed only 'Stourton Bassett' in your own hand, *S – Clare tells me that your dear wife's long ordeal is over. I think I know of this complexity and depth of grief and I dare to share it just a little. – E.*

From Clare's copying ploy I acquired your email address, Evie. Now by email I could tell you in perfect blandness that I intended accepting Clare's dates. The eighth to the twenty-first. Today was the seventh. *I promise not to panic* – over what has lain between us, Evie, unresolved.

Clare sensed a hermetic impulse. Neither I nor Evie would dare admit to the indestructibility of love until one of us came to be widowed. What alchemy is this, Evie, with your old confidante Clare, that she should sense beneath the hide – beneath the crust – what we require to believe ourselves to be, if the living of one's life is to remain manageable.

Need I swear to myself on what I hold holy that there's no collusion between the two of you on this? There's not a scintilla of calculation in you, Clare. You *sensed*. But also it was your will to find out whether the magnitude of what you had witnessed in Evie when we were amid the dreaming spires could indeed prove illusion; ephemerality; an infatuation. For you, Clare, needed to believe in Evie's love for me. Evie set the marker for you as to what love could be. That was Evie's role with you: to set you markers. That was the big one you'd not attain to, and somehow knew you never could or would. You would hurry past that region of human experience in your friend Evie. Yet all this while you have needed to know, however vicariously, that this love was – would always be – authentic: that, at Oxford, when it struck crisis and struck us dumb, it was unfinished.

This is the hidden impulse that has had you bringing the two of us back together on this foreign soil. You also are complicit with us within the hem of the cloak of this illimitable wood that smothers the Villa Les Maures.

'You need fresh vistas, Simon,' so you said, 'but among old friends.'

You cannot have intended as 'vista' this malign forest on a moonblanked, starless night, all expectation gone of reaching the villa this side of morning! And suddenly, now, with that prospect evaporated, with no contriving any consistent route to any other human habitation in this imminent inky blackness, no conceivable coherent course to take until the sun rises again on this lost place, to escape these trees interminable (subservient to the demon of their chaotic terrain) – the realisation descends upon me as a whirlwind sweeps an oak … *that you, Clare, have known what Evie and I have not admitted to ourselves – that she and I love each other beyond any means of measurement, and for ever. You have been acting not from knowledge or calculation, but from divine perceptive instinct.*

I stop, I touch a holm-oak's crusted trunk; my knees tremble and I am sitting now, here at its roots. And this tree, and in the face of its master, I clutch this secret which you, Clare, have exposed to us – to Evie and to me. It has lain and lurked, inadmissible until this strange moment lost in the labyrinth of this forest!

Are we not amazed, Evie, you and I, at this vast truth's exposure to us? Buried so long ago, grown over, the site of it forgotten, the spot untraceable! It is as if, when the whirlwind strikes, a great oak topples and under its wrenched roots is revealed the gleaming chalice.

Here it lies, vivific Evie! Even as I sit on this steep ground beside the ragged holm, the self-same treasure-truth visible only to me and to you, a chalice-Excalibur. For this is a grail that is defence against the present Evil. It is beyond the imaginative compass of your spouse across the room (pottering about for what to take with him on this little holiday with your old Oxford crony Clare). He can't trouble us. You have been true to him in his fashion, Evie, and always will be, nearly two decades his junior and lighting no fires in you. He has his world, where you play your part to perfection, so competent, decorative, *au courant*, everybody's names on your tongue and their bits of flattering significance at your fingertips like canapés. You have given him Gyles as heir, your womb declining further impregnation. You're protective of his self-esteem, and *fond* of him. Don't dare be fond of me. Keep your fondness to nurture Victor's fondness for himself in ermine.

That tremor of panic of yours was at our secret being exposed not to him but to ourselves. Yet now it has been revealed, this golden chalice. On this instant I know myself to have the weapon against the force of evil that has made a hostage of me. I have this demon of despair at bay. If I am to be destroyed it will not be without a fight. Perfect love, a voice of wisdom says, casteth out fear. I have no fear.

This moment at which I know fear to be gone from me, ho! ... there is conjured out of nothing, out of darkness and silence, a rush of wind, barbarous and shrill, that has me hunched in astonishment against a trunk. In thirty seconds it is gone again to silence! What does this portend?

A mistral girding itself?

Summons to be done with me?

Now with no trace of daylight left, the darkness is impenetrable and black the very sky. Should I now get low, follow my elementary ploy of keeping to the lowest ground, pressing on, to attempt escape by any route from whatever the forest can visit upon me? Yet I know that is not simple. These dry gullies are so thick with vegetation and fallen limbs that to walk in virtual blindness in dense growth is the surest way of putting out an eye.

Advance, with a hand before the face. I am bucklered by a cup of gold.

I sense a fall in temperature. There is a whispering of branches, challenge mounting.

Here is your hand unseen in mine, Evie ... The daemon of this forest will have seen it. Yet nothing outwardly will have changed from this exposure. The distance between Oxford and Warwick will have grown shorter. We may not rush to bed, my darling, you and I, though Eros will deny us nothing. *Nous aimons chacun l'autre. C'est la vérité, c'est vérité.* You hear me, Evie – I lower my voice, not raise it. We love one another, you and I, melting beyond the presumption of human loving. And listen, Evie – hear me on what is known anew to us and to the savage master of this wood: this re-admitted love has ungelded faith in God and by means of its admission embraces all. I am restored to a lost ability ... Marigold is whole again, and truly to be mourned for what she has ever been and ever striven to be.

I am astonished. You, Evie, by your enchantment in this black forest, you have clad me in the armour of love in the faith which makes for hope. Thus armoured I can invoke unprecedented healing, wholing, pushing back the devil of this place. It is behovely. Out of desire in our dark garden we become one flesh. It is behovely.

Totus tuus sum. We have lived too long with our Creator's treasure buried. Let there be lust, that there may be love. For thus the race of men is made. In lust's love is our being. Here is the bonding of the poles, female and male, in mutual amorality, mutual despoliation, surrender, melting of self. This is the rightful bestowal, the rightful impulsiveness, the blind green snake that squirms and is despised and lives in and by concealment and bruises the heel. Without green lust we shall unlearn the principle of love and unlearn life's peaceful motive.

There is no righteousness without our sin committed and admitted, no light without this dark embraced, no hope without all ambition drowned by consummation, no wholeness without nothingness attained, no spirit without body celebrated by faith in love.

Three indeed are present in this threatening wood – Evie, I, and the daemon of this place.

What is that sound now, like a distant surge?

It is wind rustling, high up among the summits of these jumbled peaks. And now it's here, fierce among the compliant treetops that flank the gully where I am crouching from the cold. Instantly it has swept these trees and is already gone … and yet a bigger, further, sound is persistent now and swelling. It is Satanic forces mustering.

Evie, Evie, for those first dismaying weeks after we had met and were transfixed by love at that Bullingdon ball, were we not chaste? Our chaste restraint was in devout ratio to the force of the wonder. What *was* this thing? This totality of possession? This command for which anyone might surrender *life*? You had turned nineteen – and I at twenty-one already unchallengeable as to manhood in full Adamic flower.

Right now, here, in this menacing forest, we are rediscovered afresh in chaste innocence.

Clare, you were already my chosen companion at our table for the ball to come after the end of Hilary term when one of our group's quartet of girls dropped out and word went forth for a replacement: that very evening I was escorting you at the term's end OUDS production of Cymbeline at the Playhouse. At once you had our requirement.

I'll bring a friend. You trust my judgment.
Of course. Who?
Another botanist. On my staircase.
Ah. Reading flowers. She has a name?
Evie.
Of the garden of Eden.

Just so. But fully clothed. She needs her circle widened.
My raffish band …
She'll take the risk. She's no family in England. They're always faraway
and on the move. Dad's in Shell.

That was your brief to me, Clare: as Tristan was briefed to ready Isolde for marriage to another, or Paolo to entertain his brother's bride by sharing ancient tales, I was to broaden a first year student's circle.

Your thrusting mama, in Parliament and widowed, was not going to leave her only child on any shelf or imperfectly matched. She had propelled you into the social whirl, populated your world with the best of the crop, among whom I was scarcely to be counted, being unlanded and untitled, as she once carelessly reminded me at a tennis party on the Horsham circuit where you and I in our teens biffed balls in school holidays. Yet you were drawn to me, Clare: I made you laugh, you thought me reckless yet contrarily 'felt safe' with me, you said, joining me at Oxford in my second year and latching on to me as your steady. With your new-found fellow disciple of Botany and Biological Sciences on the same staircase at LMH above the meandering Isis, you sought to encircle a disciple of Italian and the Classics and Petrarch, Boccaccio and Dante.

In that Beatrician inspiration with which your companion possessed my inner being on first encounter, the brief had gone with the wind. Here was one, of immediate allure, unaware, in whom diffidence veiled daring and linking them humour which awaited another's sharing … and melting. By the instantaneity of mutual recognition, that other was surely to be I. Our eyes met, and knew. Our eyes spoke for our lips. To know was to love … The flicker of guilt at your confidante's upstaging of you who had brought us together that Spring night amid the Chiltern hills was made to vanish by your sheer generosity … Look, Clare, now, at this endowment of yours: how natural, how instinctive, how a further three decades and more of life and death and the wisdom or unwisdom of experience your constant generosity is by way of reuniting us.

Then, virgin to virgin, we three shared the wisdom of innocence. It was Evie you counselled: 'We cannot lose our virginity twice' – so Evie quoted you to me. And when you did lose yours, Clare – so inconsequentially with that South African rugby fellow from BNC – a membrane was pierced that left you closed, perhaps, for ever.

Yet, Evie, when in the end or the beginning you Eved me, *that* was far from inconsequential, far from *closing*. Our sin was ordained; seraphic and secret. None but Clare so much as had an inkling of the power of such wonder: she stood agape. Supremely alone we lived its wonder. Nakedness was our unique discovery. We were pre-birth, and hence immortal, in Eve-Adam union.

Is that not so, my darling? None knew besides Clare. You and I could not have endured the talk of the town. We had no vows but the vows our bodies made. The scent of you wrapped us. Out of the bosom of innocence we loved in astonished innocence. Our joy defied comparison. It was we uniquely who had discovered what love was – each to become our *nothing* in the other, and thereby everything. For us to fall in love was a falling out of the dimensions such as mystics told of in words no less ours than theirs.

Could we have known of the trap: the pit dug for us? I was reading the *Inferno* of Dante's wild imagination during my final term while you still had a year to go.

What of Paolo and Francesca, cursed by their bliss and blessing cursed? Could it be that our bodies could usurp the very purpose of our love?

What when the body was spent and husked? Was body's ardour to consume its owner's love? What was this spectre of unmeaning? My tutor-priest Paul of Pusey House, within his vow of celibacy asks if I am not to marry you, and I hear my own voice in reply that we had not come together as prospective parents but as lovers. What involuntary response was this: whose voice has spoken it? I heard my own arrogance, my sheer self-satisfaction ... as if any man of God was denied knowledge of what I knew. I catch the fleeting sadness of his frown as if he is seeing God's design baulked by inferior vanities ... as if a shaft of *eros* had spiked the creative endorsement of love.

Truly our bodies had made their vow, Evie. Yet then that terrible impasse. The only *spoken* vow we would make was the parting vow. I was at sanity's limit. If I was not to slide into outright madness it could only be by unchaining us both to re-possess that previous life we had each lived before all we had known in one another's arms.

In pale immobility you offered the proposition – *pleaded*, though you checked yourself – that we should take a long-Lent pledge of chastity, a 'body-fast' you said, for whatever penitentiary spell my Furies required of us ... but that we would not break utterly.

You listened to my silence.

Then you said,

'Is it Paul you have been talking to?'

'Paul doesn't even know we make love.'

'Of course he knows.'

I am gazing out from your first-floor window in your rooms at LMH onto lawns and river. When I turn you are soundlessly in tears.

There was no acceptance: you were stunned. I gave no option of reprieve. I was at sanity's limit, I did not know what had overtaken me. I chose to take your silence for acceptance, as if at a guilty verdict upon an innocent in the dock.

What was I doing? In heaven's name, what was I doing? The merest doubt cast on our love had always turned you silent – even a passing jest: *that* I had observed. Did I not know this? In love we had met and matched, and met-and-matched we were larks mounting. You were mischief, dare-devil, zest and all vitality; you were joy, you were peace. Our love inhabited our centre, 'corolla' was your word: modesty, pliancy, beauty; sacred fire and tremulous peace. Yet simultaneously it was that crimson bed of the sick rose. Suddenly – in a matter of hours – its unassailability was in fearful hazard, its peace fled, gone wild, innocence illusory. I, so full of fear, had stumbled into my own Inferno, the equivalent of death without the privilege of oblivion. We conjoining, that alone made all that counted life. Oh, we were lust, and proven beauty, and in our triumph nothing was loveless or alone. It had been all that earth required, until the day it cracked. I saw the fissure, and mesmerised watched it widen. What could I do?

It cracked open, spewing, as if the physical brain of man by which mind and soul and heart had ever come to be recognised and honoured, worked upon and exalted was sludge, to be sponged off as nothing. For him who had known exaltation there was nothing now but madness, blindness, death. I was mad. Wilfully I had taken your answering silence as assent.

Clare descended upon my rooms at Worcester in trembling dismay. She had received a letter from your mama in Oman. She had the letter in her hand, entreating enlightenment from one her parents knew as their daughter's closest friend at Oxford.

'What am I to tell them, Simon? That suddenly you have gone mad? Out of a clear blue sky? They are intelligent people, Simon. I know them. I've stayed with them in Dorset.'

I replied, 'The Furies. They give no warning.'

'What happened, Simon? You were so happy ... blissful. Evie ... you – equally.' You are on the ottoman under my window, clutching the letter. 'She says Evie can give no coherent explanation. You spoke of Blake ... '

I had grasped at Blake in impending turmoil, at the *Marriage of Heaven and Hell* in its celebration of human energy and sexuality, at the *Songs of Innocence and Experience*.

I quoted the strange poem, *O Rose thou art sick. The invisible worm, that flies in the night in the howling storm, has found out thy bed of crimson joy, and his dark secret love does thy life destroy.* 'I know what it means.'

You waited, Clare.

I began, 'The act of love ... '

'In the crimson bed ... '

'Suddenly it became a tyrant. An end in itself. An insult to all we had known. Suddenly. A tyrant. That consummation uplifting us, endorsed our joy. I can see no way out, Clare.'

It was a grievous interchange. I added only, 'Don't let her go under. Like me.'

Within days, my Evie, I was in wild subjection to the Furies, in a manner you could only know of, never know: none could know, not even tutor Brother Paul – I was finished off, fit for death: having done my studying I sat my Finals as an automaton of borrowed learning, and flit our university. Clare was at once your protectress: that I knew. It was a whole year later, on my return to London from Singapore, that you found me, Clare, and insisted on calling to see me. We were to meet at the Palio on Earls Court Road, near to my digs next to the Poetry Society. I approached our encounter with an ardent dread, unable to plan what I might dare speak of. In the event, it could not be of Evie, could it? You told me only that she would have scuppered her Degree 'but for her capacity for constructive panic'.

'By constructive panic are our fates determined,' I replied. But few are endowed with Evie's grit.

I was drinking a vodka *stenggah*, Singapore-fashion. I did not enquire why 'panic' should still have been present a year after I had quit Oxford and disappeared far abroad. My mouth was blocked from asking of you anything about Evie. I could give you not the smallest message for her. You knew that, Clare. Even so you found space to say, 'You took her to that island like Elvira Madigan and had walked with her into the woods and shot her, and then yourself.' Then you fell silent, looking into your Heineken.

And there that line of talk ended, as if by a bullet, or two bullets. Since I could not bear to hear anything of Evie we spoke of you and your lordly suitor who was dazzling you. I scarcely wished to speak of myself, and when you said 'A career in advertising?' I could answer only with an empty tremor of the head at the notion of a calling to inconsequence. My eyes were on your fingers around your glass of lager, fingers as precise as Evie's by the precision of dismembering of flowers.

What had I perpetrated, my Evie?

I am brought up sharp in this black wood ... stock still. What love-murder was this of mine, done in the impossibility of what we imagine for mortal love? Is it only now, here, in this place, an avenger has found us out, isolating me from the troupe, intent on harrying me to death.

I am sick with alarm, motionless on this blind track. *Yet each man kills the thing he loves.* My insane conviction as to what was demanded of us became your acquiescence, in modesty and pliancy, until 'constructive panic' secured survival.

Stock still, on this track, *quia amore langueo.* O my Evie. How our betrayals never let us go.

I sense the forest hunching. *The way in is the way out.* Such I taught myself, long ago. What did I mean? I hear another voice, faintly, *Pour out, that you may be filled.* It is Augustine. '*Learn not to love that you may learn to love.*' Are you not, saint, speaking of love by supersession – losing self, emptying, kenosis, opening upon wonder? Did not your God, Augustine, give life to the lad of flesh and blood so as to trump it?

What was once in me as prior wisdom stemmed from my boyhood, from a vision of a paradisial vista inspired by the Grampians opening upon a new innocence to become my superseding vow to *Christ.*

At Oxford I had inhaled the odour of inferno. To save my life, Evie, *to save my life* I had let go of you. And now I'm with my fellow autobiographer Dante Alighieri, caught up in this very labyrinth of trees. I too knew Beatrice in the flesh, knew as nakedly as Mechtild of Magdeburg knew God, to meld in singleness that shared innocence of nakedness. In each and every one of us there is but one true paired singleness. Mechtild granted singleness to God, with God: let me not gainsay her. Abelard paid with his testes for divinising the coupling body. I had gelded myself of the nakedness of love, Evie, for no perceivable cause but that its consummation had consumed us; suddenly no longer realising us but nullifying, making rag-dolls of us. We had loved and must now, all at once, make a pact of love's immolation. You wept. You survived. We went where life would take us.

But now – look now, where life has brought me ... to this house party of our ancient acquaintance, the Decameron refugees from a world in wild disorder, and you on the point of joining the party, including in particular *myself*, in the company of the obsessive Florentine poet as dragoman exploring whatever in human love may ascend to the divine. Just how much did you know, my Dante, in the life you lived and were challenged by? What of life-in-the-flesh got you to recognise the promise of *eros* as of holy provenance? Its unconditionality – that no longer are there two – a woman, a man – but *one flesh*, as Paul put it? No hem, no seam.

Such is the *Gelassenheit* we had the trick of, Evie, *knowing* one another, letting-go into the melting, suddenly, by glance, touch and lip, sealed at the instant of now and ever by joy and sleep. We can't unknow what we have known. Wonder tells.

Dante, my touched genius, you write of love let loose from flesh, inspired by flesh to be lifted beyond flesh. So we presume for the figure of Jesus in whom the two of us proclaim faith. The solvent of faith is love, person to person, in the exercise of wonder.

Whee-ee-ee – here's the wind again, this time without relent. *Wha-w-aaw* – lashing us, Evie, twisting and torturing the scarcely discernible trees rooted beneath where I cower below the canopy. The high limbs of these corks protest like flagellants swishing and buffeting this way and that way. The *chataigniers* of a hundred feet loop like siege-engines amid the racket. This is the devil's Mistral, cold from the north.

We shall outlive all this, Evie, you and I. Look how we are stormed and counter-stormed. We hunker down beneath this tempest and its cold and fury. We are one another's protection: together in our forest we are indestructible. There's no fear in love; not in perfect love. Here we prove you, John, amid the ritual assault by loveless anarchy upon the rooted domain of animate earth. There is a mortal complicity here, darling – God's own earth defiant at his unleashed rage.

See how the forest dances and ducks in its battery of storming, a furious ecstasy! Leaping, lunging, orgiastic in riot and ruckus. Limbs that age has weakened crack and crash, entire trees come down, the allotted centuries of umbrella pines and chestnuts snuffed. It is the demons' yearly purgation, the ungovernable descending on this forest from permanent snows as from the soaring Ruwenzori of my own acquaintance, and its alien gods.

Here in this massif is no lightning and no Ruwenzori thunder to herald rain and hail. On my entire perambulation since mid-afternoon I've seen and heard no water at all. Nothing is known to me of the patterns of weather here beyond the wind's name, Mistral, *Masterly*, –but that it brushes the Alps and sweeps south by the valley of the Rhone, bringing no rain.

I too am likely to be parched before the master of this place has done with me.

After that terrible vow of quittance, Evie, not bearing to think of you nor even *for* you – what you went through – I was in blackness, a hollow, acting my days through, Chancing Simon Chance. Abelard, Paolo … and which uncounted others? Now this Chance, he needed to be *d'ailleurs*, somewhere else, like the French poet. He responded to an advertisement for a job in Singapore selling fertiliser. From that remove for two rootless years he watched his friends settling into their structured professions, laying the ground for future security and distinction, and glazed linen and sedate advancement to the obituary columns by way of the law, the merchant banks, ancestral acres, real estate and Lloyds of London. Politics was seldom any more for gentlemen, and the Foreign Office had gone dull.

When back in Town, insouciant, and shallow – yet not dumb, not friendless, and surviving by writing advertising copy – I'd meet up with Wally for an Italian meal. He was buying little companies to boost and sell, or strip and merge this with that. He was excited and a hero to his Violetta for his flare. Joining me at the Palio he'd bate me, 'When are you going to do a proper job?'

Julian was into the money-broking scramble at his newfangled computer network twelve hours a day, amassing tiny percentages on gargantuan sums for Warburgs. Reggie was after me to snatch a share with whatever I could lay my hands on in his latest fund with Panmure which could scarcely fail to double by Christmas. Charley was eating his dinners at the Bar. 'The law,' he'd intone, 'looks after its own and it takes no risks. It lives off the risks of others.' He was already a member of Brooks's, middle-aged and not yet twenty-four, already going to fat. And I, God knows, I was half the man I was three years before, who had loved the woman Evie. A half-man, with no calling.

I grasp a tree in the riot of the tempest, as the stark truth grasps me. Of the two great injunctions – *love God, love neighbour* – the second earns authority *only* by virtue of the first. I have lived this long and *now* I have it! The truth of the love is in its unassailability, its indestructibility, its unconditionality. In passion it is sealed. Evie neighbour-in-love, co-melder in my arms, makes this truth in no other manner than that of the holy love whereby creation entire comes to be: our bodily passion, made true by reflexion of Your ardent dispassion. By this recognition are we redeemed.

Here is my hand on the rugged skin of this cork-oak. See, Lord, your own hand in the gratuitous embedding in the cycle of reproductive life the phenomenon of love by the mechanism of gender: she receiving, he giving, by polar acclamation. *I love you!* That gratuitous bequest to your species revealed uniquely to mankind.

In this intensity of forest darkness, Evie, I see at last the two commandments in interplay such as would have saved me from the Furies.

Unless I love you first, my Lord, whether knowing so or unaware, I cannot love any other in love's *truth*.

True love leaps from the wonder of innocence. We knew that very wonder, Evie. When we met at the trees' end beyond the lake at Worcester we seemed to know the place already. Each knew the route the other had come by, a gift of prescience. We seemed to know that something was expected, and when we knew we loved neither of us was surprised but merely glad this *was* the place our blood remembered a thousand years since we were children first. The ancestral innocence was God's, first God's as gift, opening to whosoever shall love in wonder, joy and beauty recognised.

Yet when suddenly and secretly that holy innocence is blinded, when upon an instant the truth of love is betrayed by flesh to the unseen enemy, when sheer body has surreptitiously usurped the divinity that two bodies had presumed to seal in the act of love, then is a lover at the terrible mercy of the Furies. The body informs the soul. The Flesh has paired with the Devil after all, and the Devil entertains no innocence, no wonder. In culpable innocence I had led us into our *égoisme à deux*. Into the crevasse called *self* had I hurtled, locked in embrace.

What sermons does this bishop preach himself, in the howling storm! Now, now, now do I perceive what cast me into that crevasse of annihilation; how in my innocence and because of it I was blind to sight of Him who had brought us his gift of wonder, frankincense and myrrh, and had forfeited for ever recovery of it. Evie, we were so young and urgent.

How could we be aware that the wisdom of innocence is to be exposed and stifled by the wisdom of experience? Yet now that strain of prior innocence, that inkling, creeps back upon me, out of the remoteness of childhood. Wally, you and I were eleven, amid the unconjurable beauty of Rannoch and still undiscovered Ericht, when in my vision I was gazing down upon a vale of paradise from a remote ridge-top, the panorama of unassailable serenity drenched in sunlight and a yellow lakeshore along a sheen of water disappearing beyond sight: the place I knew to be the soul's destination. It is as if now, my Lord, that in the savage forest I am thinking back to what I had supposed irrecoverable.

Since entering school, had I not sung in choirs? Now I was again singing. What choirs sing is the inherited faith, as love and awe and lamentation interchangeably. My Augustinian pilgrimage, secret and unwilled, set me on the path to priesthood, the path to a second innocence, a primal trust.

My Bambuti said, *Trust the forest and it will repay your trust.*

You will have somehow known, Evie, of my vocational itinerary: it will not have astonished you; it may even have flattered you.

So then it was you sent me – had me sent, you providing your list-assembler my name and old address – the formal invitation to your marriage, embossed in cursive script, in its vellum envelope, to a landed figure of the Tory party, Member for some piece of Warwickshire, already forty-something and you not much more than half his age. One knew the fellow's name. A grandee county marriage with a mate high-chested on his territory.

I could not attend any such marriage. I might send a mere courteous refusal: it was to be just three weeks before my passing out of Cuddesdon and my formal ordination as priest of the Church of England. Yet I did not quite do that: I chose, did I not, Evie, to telephone your old home number – chose without reflection. And it was your voice that answered, you of the 'five voices': it was voice number one, brisk, assertive.

'Who is this?' – 'this', the newly fashionable American way.

Ah. And you were alone. That I knew at once.

'I wanted to congratulate you on your engagement. But I cannot come to your wedding.'

A pause.

'I understand.' Already it was voice three.

A further pause.

'I reckoned you would.'

'I needed you to know. There will be a lot of old friends. Oxford, naturally.'

'Of course.'

Now a longer pause.

'Listen,' you say. 'May I not see you?'

'How?' I ask.

These accumulating pauses.

'I am thinking, London.' There is that in your voice – the muted woodwind.

'When?'

'Sort of Friday or Saturday.' The secret *pianissimo* of old swirled upon me. You name the adjacent dates. 'I shall be in London buying things, checking wedding lists.' The strings have entered. You say you'd be staying at your brother Eddie's flat in Ennismore Gardens. 'We could rendezvous there, in the evening,' of the Friday, that was.

Ennismore Gardens would not be more than fifty minutes from Cuddesden Theological College on the Berkshire border.

'I'll take you out to dinner,' I say.

'You can stay the night … if it's easier.' It was voice four. It has outflanked anything I might have said about the imminence of my ordination.

Today her brother Eddie can surely no longer have that world-of-its-own top-floor studio whose huge window scans northwards to the green of the Park between the tree-lined ascent of the street. There Eddie lived in imaginative disorder. That evening he was not to be there; not arriving, not expected. You wore a black pencil dress, fitting mute with a bow – somewhere there was a bow – and that same scent which at Oxford we had named *Francesca's*.

At dinner in the little place on the corner of Trevor Square you replied to the question you could not but be asked, namely whether you loved your imminent lifelong partner.

'Enough,' you answer. There is a proximity of tears. Yet your eyes are also full of courage. Courage you always had, in both its shapes: pluck, and fortitude. You do not quail at challenge, least of all a challenge you set yourself.

'He knows about us?'

'That I had a regular date at Oxford – a man at Worcester. Yes.'

In that quick glance, behind the courage I do see sorrow. (Just now, Evie, I have beaten sorrow into joy, as sword to ploughshare.)

'You go to bed with him.' I did not allow it to be a question.

'Not a lot,' you returned. 'His body bores me.'

That night, did we not love as angels? In the supreme exclusivity of bodily knowledge one of another and unassailable by Furies? Nothing was spoken: about ourselves, nothing spoken whatsoever.

In that purification, Evie, was I ordained. That momentary angelic repose was a catharsis of what had gone before. Celibacy was now apt. All that while since Oxford I did not claim you, I did not crave you. You belonged to a previous mode of being wherein life was shared, was virtually created by us, which we had the right to make to disappear. It was as if you had died, or do I mean, each of us had died; yet somehow we had lived on, aware of a previous life while accepting that whatever we had known was irrecoverably other. Whatever I was with you, or you were with me, had been then and thus: we were writ in water, a shadow in the wood. So I wrote at the time. Subsequently not merely was celibacy apt but chasteness too. And not merely apt. I would have myself suppose I had moved beyond body and what body might bestow upon further negation on behalf of the domain of the soul in union with God: beyond all the draping of image and allegory. *Beyond being! Beyond knowing!* Thus the Meister spoke of that innermost dark and silence, the true ground from which the soul's spark flies to illumine paradise ... and not easily accessible paradise! What else was the source of my calling? There was that fragment of verse to which I would resort at Cuddesdon

Where there was nothing there is God: the word
Came to my mind: it might have been a flower
Dropt from a rainbow ...

... such a flower of kenosis with which I was acquainted, in the exercise of obeisance. I speculated that my calling was to take the vows not of priest but monk, in conviction

laying myself open to You
laying my self open to your presence
laying my soul in and upon You
laying open to You in your nothingness
in my depth and in my height.

VII

How was it that after my ordination the aptness of celibacy, cathartic denial of the self, clouded? – the body now irrelevant or aloof.

I would not be monk, yet I would be chaste and meanwhile work the world, the demands of ministry and also of the dying, the lost, those bereft of love, strangers to love, unknown by joy, beauty-blind, uncomprehending of my truth, Truth itself. Thus there gathered around me all the clutter of the this and that as Bishop's chaplain and curate of Holy Trinity, the pettifogging functions. Petty, fogging …

You got wind of my engagement. That surprised me. You wrote me a card, referring to Marigold as 'your musician'. How did you know of her profession? At Oxford you'd speak of your flowers as virgin births while I spoke of melodies.

Almost immediately Marigold followed me to Africa to be

married in the mudbrick cathedral of St Paul's, Kasese, on the Uganda side of that wild Congo frontier. It was across the frontier with the Congo in the vast Ituri forest that my prospective charges inhabited and delved. Relentlessly they were being encroached upon by Bantu, for ever creeping across the continent river by river from two thousand years ago, planting yams and claiming any land they could break the soil of. With their metal and their cloth they bartered for pygmy-trapped bushmeat and pygmy-gathered medicine. The Church's Bantu priesthood and converts could not but look upon pygmies as an inferior species of creation beyond the redemption of gospel and the Faith. I knew well enough their exclusion meant their withering and dying from the necrosis of game reserves and tourists. The CMS had been casting around for an outsider prepared to reach them. That meant a white man. *That* was the challenge that caught me, a challenge to overlay primal innocence with Christian innocence. 'That alone,' I have told Marigold, 'might save them from extinction. Don't you see? It is a complex test of the faith I claim.'

We are again in Holy Trinity. You say nothing and on the instant I wonder if what I am saying makes any sense.

'I'll be going out to Uganda's border with eastern Congo in the spring attached to the regional Anglican diocese.'

My church on Prince Consort Road is growing dark. The stained glass prophets softly glow high in the west windows. The place has remained held by a strange silence, poised for an intensity of worship. You and I have been speaking in a whisper. The nursery school beyond the north wall has packed up for the day. In an hour I will be conducting the eucharist, spoken in formal intimacy: a mere handful will attend.

I get up to light four huge candles, two at each end of the altar on either side of two exquisite sprays of flowers of which I would once have required of myself to name each bloom.

When I return to the row of chairs, you are sat very upright, gazing at the candles with that penetrating concentration that is your hallmark. It comes upon me that if I have failed to convince you of my African intention and its Christian premise – the fountainhead of what I have come to believe – it will augur badly. I need your approval. You have become compelling, a touchstone of my authenticity, as if my inner conduct requires this admirer's endorsement.

You turn back to me as if startled by my presence. 'There you are!' Beside you.

I say, 'People don't come to Christianity by having it explained to them.'

'That I understand. Something has to happen first.'

I take your hand, your bow hand, and am reminded of the perfection of your skin and the astonishing precision of your fingertips. I ask if you would like to come with me to Africa when your course is complete.

'Come with you,' you echo in a whisper.

'I suppose we'd have to marry. If you could bear that.'

Our eyes have met, and with me shocked at myself we are on the point of an embrace. Lips have all but met when you shoot a glance at the altar and its leaping backdrop. 'We are not alone!' you hiss, blushing wildly and pulling back while gripping my hand with ferocity.

I have frozen in alarm. Your eyes have dropped from the figure of Jesus crucified to the chequered marble of the chancel floor, ruthlessly hard.

'You met your Jesus – ' this was Marigold-the-defiant whispering – 'in the desert. What made for this desert?'

The suddenness of the change in you is like a blow to the side of the head.

How much of the truth dare I expose to *myself*, let alone to you? You know next to nothing of my time at Oxford, nothing more than that I had studied Dante, and had what I presumed to call a girlfriend.

I take cover in a part of the truth. Of what predicated my own void I cannot speak. I reveal only one thing that spurred me into seeking the bond with Christ.

'My sister,' I begin falteringly. That there were just the two of us, she knew, how we were always close, Lucy and I – Lucy looking to me for the boundaries of her very self when the family split. I was always the definer, even when I was five and she two. We'd grown up familiar with a sort of C of E Christianity, a Mrs-do-as-you-would-be-done-by line of conduct. We were never doctrinal subscribers. It was patently half-myth – the story – with the snake-oil of eternal life thrown in. Father imbibed it as a child and never questioned it. What we had ran in the blood, the Tory party in the kneeling position.

'Lucy had a boyfriend at seventeen. We knew his family pretty well. We played tennis, rode each other's horses. At twenty she was formally engaged. He was twenty-four. She got pregnant, then he dropped her. I was in Singapore and came home. Lucy had an abortion – at four months, almost five, made legal only on the grounds that she was suicidal. I was a formal witness as to her state of mind. I was at her side, in the Hammersmith hospital. In the ward the nursing staff avoided looking at me. I saw the foetus they had been obliged to kill. This was to have been my niece. My unworthiness as a brother pierced me. I was no source of clarity, no source of strength. I had no reserve of courage. I was pretending. I began making my living writing advertising copy – women's lingerie and Mars Bars. The more highly I was regarded the more disgusted I was at the abuse of any capabilities I had. The lingerie copy was crafted to make the frills and chiffon alluring enough for more young women to get pregnant and be betrayed.'

I was stopped there by a stab of honesty. Did I not know about betrayal!

You caught my eye.

'So I went back to Dante. You could say, Dante came back to me. I took a room in Wakefield to return to my old tutor. Paul is a monk.

He was attached to Pusey House when I was at Oxford, following the Augustinian discipline. Now he had joined Mirfield's Community of the Resurrection in Yorkshire. I found myself reading the *Commedia* as if entering the mind of Dante was a matter of life and death. Then I discover Paul to have long held to the Christian story as metaphor – my word, not his. He spoke of "divine algebra". He was hardly concerned as to historicity: for him, faith on the part of his namesake Paul and the apostles, and all who have followed, validated the figure of Christ as an exposition of Truth for ever – truth with a big T. Brother Paul was speaking of the gospel story as the algebra through which to work the Truth he breathed as *faith*. Paul does breathe his faith: the gospel is his oxygen. Jesus saw himself as parable, taught in parable, lived and died as parable. You may call it art. Paul would say, "We in life are all players in the great allegory which Jesus realizes and transcends." He renders Man unique in all creation.

'For me the implausibility had floated away. Jesus stood forth as a living reality. I had converted, Marigold. It took my breath away. It was as if a prior wisdom had had the veil snatched away: a pristine revelation, utterly simple.'

There we were, side by side at Holy Trinity, I retailing my secret innermost narrative for the first time to anyone, innermost narrative to a non-believer.

You're still gazing at the floor. You say,

'Your life changed … '

'Yes.'

'In a day … '

'In an hour.'

'An hour!'

The vast unspeakable secret of our Christian Church had been spoken. It taught *metaphor*. So it had ever taught. Gospel truth that spun its metaphor like a silkworm out of its Truth Inexpressible. Your head makes a tiny jerk. 'Not truth at all! … but *metaphor*.'

'Was it ever any different?'

You are speechless.

'God is a word. Which he does not seek. Yet in the unwanted word man can alone encounter him.'

I have lost you. It is a risk I must take for my own faith's sake.

'God takes form for the sake of man. It was always like this.'

'So he sent Jesus.' This is you telling me: I can hear the words surprise the speaker.

'To make the relationship real,' I say.

'In time? In a place?'

'And in eternity. And infinity.' It is the grand encompassing parable of the Church. 'When I unveiled it as metaphor, I could believe.'

Our silence is pierced by the cry of Jesus from the cross of the great window that governs the church we are alone in, *Eloi, Eloi, lama sabbachtani!* Why my God hast thou forsaken me? – the cry of destitution crucial to the revealing of the truth Jesus was and is dying for.

No one before has ever spoken to you in this sort of language.

'It cannot be otherwise – because of the mind of man, the tools we are restricted to. We deal in what we call Truth. Words and things aren't enough on their own. They must be allowed to escape dimension through what they signify.'

'Jesus was a historical figure.'

'Yes. A troublesome preacher they decided to execute. His life story in real time became *parable.*'

'He came back to life.'

'In a manner of speaking. The evangelists all make that point. *In a manner of speaking.* He walked through doors.'

'What manner of speaking?'

'A manner of experiencing, a manner of seeing.'

'Of seeing?'

'It is hard to doubt the genuineness of the apostles' encounter with Jesus after the crucifixion. They spent their lives preaching the resurrection. Several died for doing just that.'

She could hear me endorsing my faith.

I never sought to convert you, Marigold. It was as if I needed you as my own vessel of disbelief. I would, rather, bring you face-to-face with what has others letting go into belief.

'Put it like this, Marigold. Any thing in the throat of the speaker begins as a sound, a noise. From that noise the mind conjures an image of an object. An idea, maybe. A story. What gives an object its actuality is what it signifies. The truth of anything exists for the receiver of that truth. For her. For him. Whoever has been vouchsafed that truth by means of metaphor. Look' – and I tug at a piece of my cassock – 'my metaphor. The metaphor of my cloth.'

The great window resumes its contemplative presidency.

'And Africa?' you ask quite meekly.

'That was to come. Later. What was fixed in me was the simplicity of the revelation. The mighty proxy. I couldn't let go of that. Then purely by chance – grace, we would say – I heard of the opportunity to go back to where mankind began: that first garden, discovering himself to be naked, aghast at what it entailed for him.'

'The nakedness … '

'On the acquisition of consciousness. The terror of his isolation. The *I*. The mortal *I* which must go mad unless … unless one falls down in worship, declares one's love, one's gratitude for the gift of creation.'

'Music.'

'Man alone, of all species, engages in creation for its own sake. God, and Man. So music. The drum. The melisma. The song. The dance. The scored rockface, scarcely accessible, the graven image, the painted image. Worship. Love. The beauty of the truth of self-release, self-sacrifice. Jesus died for it, for the beauty of his love for us. And so the stunned joy of the resurrection. This is no banality.'

Silence holds us.
'What became of Lucy?'
'She's in the Priory.'
'A nun?'
'With a habit of drugs.'
My jest was inept and unintended.

Marigold, Marigold – how ardently in Bantu Africa you learned the tribal instruments! With what inventiveness! The men watched you uncomprehendingly. They knew only the lap-top harp and two-stringed *enenze* and tuned bow and only as accompaniment to ballad whose meaning was beyond you and often ribald. Instrumental music was for men, and their women did not know what kind of person, so contained within herself, had come among them.

Beyond, across the frontier and across the river, in the interminable forest, my pygmies were to conjure wilder sounds, quite other intensities such as would leave their mark for ever.

At our great marimba of tuned logs, laid out on parallel banana stems above the compound's patch of communal earth, you did not dare squat down among the men to go at it hammer and tongs, rippling improvisation across the compound. You did not dare. None of the African women performed on the *endara*-marimba or dreamt of doing so. But once when you looked across at that all-male music, which could go on for an hour without a break, it was with a glance of exalted guilt at the temptation to join them, let yourself go into the intoxication of it all. And at that moment you were instantly alluring, vulnerable, inviting, on the brink of self-revelation, suddenly exposed to a force you could not control or command: a counter-force to that you had striven for and which had won your fellows' respect.

You saw me catch that glance of shameful thrill and all that lurked behind it, the long narrow road of striving, of keeping to the beat, the imposition of being white among blacks, of apology for belonging to the dominant culture that had already outgrown the facile convictions that had first brought the white man here and to whose rituals and sanctimonies the natives so childishly cling. In that glance I glimpsed the maenadic beauty I had sensed in you at our first encounter caught up by what we then were hearing of Anton Bruckner and performing at the foot of the cross in the grief of Pergolesi's *Stabat Mater* such as led to the inescapable error of our marriage.

You saw me recognise that glance, and in the very reading of it, love you. Yet you would not, could not join the men in their musical work upon the *endara*, twelve-handed on the compound floor.

You look away. The sound ripples like dancing liquid across the compound and clustered dwellings, across equatorial Africa.

You were pregnant with Jasper and the thought entered that the approaching demand of giving birth would unrivet you and give you African wings. For there was Khavaïru, dominant figure of that *ensemble* and the native community, performing the collective instrument for your enchantment and enticement, ready to make a space for you on the self-same logs from which he was fountaining forth his music.

Then from behind me where I was standing on the edge of the compound stepped the diminutive figure of Agnes, your favourite, our sacristan's daughter whom you had nursed through her last, near-fatal bout of malaria. She was carrying your violin case in her bent arms like an offering. She must have slipped into our bungalow and found it by the piano in our living room. Your gaze was turned away as Agnes approached the liquid *endara*, three men or boys on each side, and the vast forest below stretching infinitely westwards, the true heart of equatorial Africa in its primal secrecy. From that impenetrability were the tuned *endara* logs provided, hewn by the sole fleeting inhabitants, the pygmies, my spiritual charges. By those iroku marimba logs was their existence evidenced among my Bantu hosts here amid the foothills of our mountains, and by the early morning fingers of smoke that rose randomly out of the oceanic canopy of trees.

Agnes' arrival with your violin surprised you. She laid beside you the instrument by which you had already brought enchantment to her and other children of our host community of Bundibughyo. I could not tell whether the child caught your remote smile as your glance rose from the black leather box you found on the hard earth at your feet. On her return I motioned to the child to bring the bow too.

And at that moment as Agnes came by me with the bow in her hands, I was gripped by a prayerful poignancy of vision of your weaving from the improvisation of your soul and fingers out of the unstoppable cascade of percussive *endara* a flow of melody that would combine in one declaration of love this entire universe of African creation from the heave of Valhalla mountains and their dazzling glaciered peaks behind us to the east, where there was thunder, to the forest darkness impenetrable to the west of us. Now at your feet, Marigold, it seemed to me, lay that device of manipulated wood and gut and tautened horsehair precisely to meet the opportunity of our bizarre incumbency at this place at this moment. I watched you bend and open the case, bring out the instrument, put it to your chin, instinctively tune the fifths of its four strings, and gazing down now not upon the *endara*-marimba but towards where the mountains lay back, hiding their summits, draw back your bow. Agnes has come beside me, watching.

Khavaïru had observed you and redoubled his own musical endeavour to be your orchestra. Yet nothing came forth from you – no sound at all. There were only tears. I could glimpse them gathering, clouding your sight of the mountains. The poised bow-hand dropped. My prayerful vision hung in the air: I was all but incredulous and tearful myself. For it had been surely a moment God-given and to have come and gone … as a meteor of divine intervention may burn out in the atmosphere before it reaches earth. I turned away at once, fearful that you might have caught me noticing your tears, fearful of an unwanted intrusion, my darling, amid this alien place of my vocation, fearful of love exposed not as beauty but viscera.

That evening you withdrew to the prayer-room which also served as your practice room. And there you performed a partita of J S Bach entirely alone, and to perfection, so as to be alone without any audience whatsoever but in the presence of music as it were of God.

The drum, the male imperative, leaves you in awe.

'They pray with the drum, Simon'.

Yes, yes. The outer *and the inner.* You are so close to the point.

From Christ you would resolutely hear no call. He was for me and my flock, not you. Music did for holy incarnation in your creative order. *Pray with the drum. Ruminate with the enzenze.* In our faith-clamouring community, you alone could not surrender to our parable or speak our metaphor. You would not mouth an invocation as elemental as Jesus' *Our Father.* In our narrow home I prayed alone. The community of Christians at our Bantu hq, Uganda-side, and my black fellow clerics, took your nursing ministrations and the literacy classes as done in the name of Jesus: Wazungu were Christians: that was a given. You were enough around the mudbrick church and mistress of a choir that sang its fantasy to blur evidence of your ducking the Bible classes and never taking a wafer. They made no remark yet noticed more than they let on. I gave up putting it to you that between reason and God was no disjunction, that out of the *lumen rationale* springs the vision where belief takes flight and makes the music that is half your repertory. You heard me and fell glum, like one tone-deaf among songsters or a castrato among the gallant. Loving me was all your daring, permitting your abduction to equatorial Africa.

When the thorns of our life snarled us, how we did turn to one another! I saw your exasperation at my faith as a subtle envy that one day would vanish. Meanwhile, what you took as Reason was your shadow. To abandon the autonomy which defined the human being at his acme on the evolutionary graph affronted you … Letting-go spelled primitive unreason, even in the act of love. When you fell pregnant I did wonder if bearing a child would release the hidden spring of blind instinctive anarchy. Just that was my thought at the baptising of Jasper when you released him into my arms over the font against the baked walls of St Mary's, Bundibughyo. When Jasper died, the mere notion of a loving Father-Creator became an outrage. That self-same deity had sacrificed her son to his Dad's vocation. It made no sense.

The drum remained, the rumination of the drum: the drum, the rippling marimba on the compound floor, the whistle-flute, the strings plucked and stroked and bowed, the shunting feet. The pygmies' cave was yet to come.

You set your heart and body against a second pregnancy.

At home on leave my old circles, they getting wind of my return – Oxford or school or county – the isolation took on another hue. How you dreaded the foregatherings. You'd tell me I became 'scarcely recognisable'. And they, the old set, meant kindly, Marigold, seeking to prise you open with their curiosity (which you took as condescension) about life in remote Congo or crossing in a dug-out a grand, urgent, secret river to delve equatorial Africa's vastest forest. They poked around for a sense of humour they began to wonder if you lacked … Clare, how particularly you sought us out, to draw in this Marigold that wed the Simon Chance you'd known so well – known as much for yourself as for your closest Oxford friend. You'd follow me into corners. Once in a corner you came out with *You don't ask about Evie, Simon.* I did not instantly respond.

'I can't really bear to know … '

What might I wish to know? Nothing. Nothing.

You half-smiled, waiting.

'If you told me she was unhappy it would distress me. If you told me she was entirely happy it would devastate me.'

'I shall not tell you, Simon. Evie does not brood. You know that. She makes the best of what life deals her. A good best. She has a young son she dotes on.'

'What made her choose her Victor?'

'She wanted to be married.'

'To Victor Goodenough?'

'He's a decent honourable man.' How intensely you were regarding me. And then you volunteered: 'She could not bear to marry anybody she might be called upon to love as she loved you.'

Marigold, Marigold, in those episodes of home leave, even the Church group – the wives and families of the CMS – found nugatory common ground. The privations of remote stations were not for sharing, swapping stories, for they were known first by Him who sent me, who 'tellest our wanderings, put our tears into his bottle'. To you, the ladies' petty pieties were ridiculous, the masks of grief at our loss of Jasper made grief phoney. You'd scurry off to your old music coteries. You'd tell them of the instruments and sound-worlds you'd found in primal equatoria they'd not a notion of.

What you might have told Evie of *me*, Clare, during that decade and-a-half when Marigold and I were alone together darkest forested Africa, in the heart of that darkness, I did not wish to know either: my blind was down. The blind was down. All those years nothing had passed between us … no word exchanged, none written; scarcely, even, was there silent, mutual speculation. *That* I knew too.

VIII

My God, this Your stormed forest is so dark.
A voice returns to me concerning You.

> 'There is in God (some say)
> A deep, but dazzling darkness; as men here
> Say it is late and dusky, because they
>   See not all clear.
> Oh for this night! where I in him
> Might lie invisible and dim.

The voice does not include the possibility of this storm overwhelming me unshriven – leaving me in cold isolation: lost in the blackness of an oceanic forest under a shrieking wind. The voice even foretells it, heralds the untraceability of one sacrificed to the spirit. How many hours to dawn? How many nights and days does the Mistral blow? I shall not ask. Let me lie invisible and dim in Him and Evie.

Up in the villa on its hilltop they will have already swerved from anxiety and concern to irritation and on to exasperation and outrage. Who is this egotistical bishop-figure to slope off and plunge the household into disorder, double the havoc of their holiday refuge already havocked by an outer world of plummeting wealth, crashing banks, reputations evaporating!

My treasured Wally, are you spinning threads from our shared childhood to weave present aberration? *Simon always pushed his luck. Swimming far beyond his depth where nobody could rescue him if he got the cramp* – swimming Loch Rannoch as ten-year-olds forever.

'That's all very well, Wally. It's too hard on Clare … '

'At least he might have told someone where he was setting off to … '

'Search-and-rescue teams don't come free … '

'Wasn't Simon done at Oxford for swimming bare-arsed across Worcester's lake?'

And with what intent have our lot worked away to prop and guile ourselves! Our distinguished ranks, our vaunted functions, our guaranteed incomes, the ordered tenor of our lives. In such proximity to Chaos! I do not exclude myself. My episcopal vesture disguises the truth of me. I am cast as one with you.

Capriciously this Simon Chance chanced to be: now let him crawl away capriciously to lie invisible like the residue of beasts hidden in this interminable density, *selvaggia e aspra e forte*. Make no searches for me, not even you Evie. I am already with you in Him. Do not disturb yourself over things past and buried by years. You are wed contentedly to your portly peer. Stay content. I am the keeper of the passion in this place.

Let the dead bury the dead and let me find my cavity to do it. I am the single human at large in this forest, its last man alive. There are dead here surely, those Maures who left this territory their African name. It can only be your entombments I have glimpsed in deepest foliage, burrowed and buried in these gully walls, you Africans, clutching your alien gods from the other side of the sea, the southern *terra*. You died here, your Baal and all his djinns unrecognised by the surrounding natives. You were a stranded race as I am a stranded man here in this unpeopled place, the very last unreasonably alive. Let me join you, Maures.

Now I quit my holm oak, I half-creep downward holding a bent forearm before my face to save my eyes from spearing twigs. High above, their fellow branches whip and writhe and sometimes crack and sunder.

I seek now only oblivion.

No more purging, no further shriving. I'll admit you djinns of the lost Moors, listen to the last whispered muezzin, an empurpled Christian of the sea's north shore. I'll make my last orison to the tutelar of this forest, malign or otherwise.

Far above I can still discern against dark sky lariats of branches twitching and lashing. At my forest's bed, darkness assembles in a hundred shades …

Did I betray you all life long, Marigold? Did I betray you by marrying you? Did I heap deceit on deceit by fathering your babies, spinning expectations, inviting mischance? When you and I fell into companionship, I was intending celibacy. I meant to put body behind me and forgo the clutter of matrimony. I knew the lure of celibacy, the *via negativa*, for priest no less than monk.

Wherever passionate response to passion is within any man's reach, such response will play the trump: *this is I, what I am for!* Such I know well enough. All at once and not invited (glimpsed at a casement window, across a crowded room, in an empty church) love catches at the heart … there is this one other.

Beatrice was that other, Dante, your heart's inspiration, object of ultimate union if not in earth then heaven, little Beatrice Portinari, ever since she was nine: when at twenty-three she was taken from this world you were left to weave her in as your consort, she *as woman*, you as *man*. On the wild route to paradise, Virgil himself gave way to her as your companion, woman in union with man in the further passion of union with a shared Lord who died and came again to life. See it anew! Beatrice did not block you from God's love, Dante, but opened you to it.

Haven't I asked myself, Marigold, whether your resistance to Christian doctrine was apprehension at one love *blocking* the other? You took on me, mission-minded, in return for having your *man*. Was that crude error?

'A man shall be joined unto his wife and they shall be one flesh.'

So Paul to his Ephesians. Yet what if all along there had been that other pairing which soul had sealed and made away with: that prior indivisibility, Man and Maker? Paul, Paul, you cannot outlaw soul for soul's caprice. *The trump had been played, the trick already taken.*

By then my mentors were persuading me that for God's will-work I was pledged for, to have a wife alongside was beyond gold. And there you were, Marigold, loving me, declaring it was me you needed.

Century upon century in a man-contrived world you women have been cast frailer than us men. So it is: frailer, yet truer. O Woman loving in the way a woman loves, you cannot but accord to the love of the man you give your body to (the sheer fact and act of it) the total of your being ... no less than the bearing of his child shall come to partake of the same totality. Thus is your being made alive and thus your love is *holy*. How can it be otherwise when in the ground of the creative ordinance you are the passive and your man the active; you await and he is awaited; man does but you *are*. And so *beyond*, you are the grander figure in this strange gendered gift of life: that within your own person you bear the totality of your being. *Unum est necessarium*, that single thing. The one commitment, Martha, *mulier*.

See how it is that, for any woman, betrayal of the love she's dared to offer forth is of infinite consequence.

You are the creatures of such infinitude. This I know.

Do you hear me, Marigold? ... and remember how, home from

Africa for good – I being attached to Southwark with a demanding brief at the CMS headquarters covering so much of Christian sub-Saharan Africa, and simultaneously at work on the *Triple Essay* on my Dante, Poet, Man and Christian – the postman brought us a certain envelope? The handwriting privily alarms me. *The Rev. and Mrs Simon Chance*: an invitation to visit Evie and her Victor for a weekend in the shires. During all those bustling leaves from our Congo diocese, neither you nor I had ever encountered Evelyn Goodenough or scarcely mentioned her. Now, however, we are 'home'.

We were to bring our twins, Evie's letter read, if we could … 'since Gyles should be here': her own son Gyles, whom Evie knew that I would know to be but a few years older than our twin girls. I might like to preach, the letter read, at their village church.

You, Marigold, at once found good reason not to be able to accept. My Oxford friends rattled you and Evie's name was writ *Oxford*. The twins on a camping holiday would not be at hand to cushion you.

You could know nothing of the roles Evie and I had played in each other's lives as undergraduates: I had never dared breathe it. I would not have trusted my voice – you, with the acutest of ears and who once had blurted to me, *If I did not have you, I would not want to live* … That particular weekend, as you briskly recalled, you had a choral composition of your own at the cathedral; you could take no chances with it.

So it was I went alone. I was expected in time for tea on the Saturday. With you on my arm, Marigold, I would have been not less but more sure of my part. Alone, I was ambushed by alarm. I took the car because of the two earlier calls I had to make that day in that Midlands diocese. After my pub-lunch I stopped by at the off-licence at the edge of Leamington and bought a half-bottle of vodka. Before reaching Stourton Bassett I pulled off the road to take a swig. I had not so much as glimpsed Evie for nearly two decades.

There she was close to the drive with an armful of hollyhocks.

Unplumed. Just as she always was, sharp-shouldered, pliant, of vital femininity.

'Put the car over there and help me with these. We've got fourteen for dinner.' No salutation, no name. She's made it a chance encounter, the responding spontaneous, sans time, of our time-less hallmark. A thick-gloved hand brushes aside a strand of hair. I take the flowers. Here is she, that same lilt of frame, the stance, the pent and tiny movements, the inexhaustible cascade of hair that grey now invades, the unconscious flagrancy of mouth.

Her eyes are on me.

'I thought you might have changed but I don't think you have. You're just well worn and presumably speak fluent African. Rugged. I like you rugged. I'm sad to have missed meeting your girls and your Marigold.'

In the house was Gyles, all but a man at 17, of whom Victor, already sixty, was so manifestly proud. Repeatedly he reverted to 'my boy Gyles'. Victor's self-assurance was not to be assailed. In his village church he sang just out of tune so loud that he must have been risking every vote in the congregation. 'God likes a voice he can hear,' he let me know. You remember, Marigold, my relaying that to you? Yet I was not to tell you of Evie murmuring to me after the service, *In church with you, I'm jealous of God.*

I preached on the Transfiguration of Christ and my namesake Simon Peter – one of but three with Jesus on that mountain top – remarking, *It is good to be here.*

There was more I could never tell you, Marigold, of that Sunday. God forbid! All of that brief weekend, with its lively dinner party on the Saturday and service on the Sunday, we had contrived, Evie and I, never to be more than momentarily alone together; whether by design or instinct or chance, thus it had been. I was aware of our performing in the presence of others a gavotte of stately partnership of which each of us was privately aware, of practised and predestined harmony which permitted no opportunity of actual bodily encounter. But then after that Sunday lunch, Evie and Gyles and I were sipping coffee on the long steps leading down into the deep garden. Victor was at the far end of it, where the trees began, beyond the blaze of Evie's shrub roses and the herbarium.

He called up to Gyles at quite a shout to join him with a bowsaw. Gyles got up to fetch the saw and go down the long lawn between the roses. How touched I had been by Victor's pride in the lad … *my boy Gyles, my boy Gyles.* He was head boy at their local public school. Gyles himself handled his papa with affectionate detachment, as if he knew the old boy couldn't refrain from playing to the full in life the script he'd written for himself, a life where everything was in place and he himself the purpose of it all.

For that moment, Marigold, the loss of our son stabbed me anew. This Gyles here was so loose-limbed, engaging a fellow, moving with the grace of latent energy. The sorrow pierced me that after the twins you would never dare to give them a sibling who might have been a brother.

Evie and I were silent, following the boy with our gaze.

I broke the silence. 'I can see something of you in him.'

'And I can see you in him.'

'How is that?'

'He is your son, Simon.'

As I turn my gaze on you, there's that tiniest of smiles playing on your lips, Evie, lips of a myriad messages. Yet *your* eyes are still on Gyles as he reaches Victor.

'Who knows?' I murmur.

'Only me. Now you.'

'You intended it?'

Now you turn to look at me with the mischief glinting alarm and with it the ancient covert invitation of intimacy.

'I had come off the pill too early. It was my bish.'

My sky has split. Beyond the sky is poised an ocean. Perhaps of tears.

Gyles is on his way back to us. He is transfigured. I am a man at once stunned and joyous. *It is good to be here.*

'And that was Tuesday,' you say, cutting the cackle with the code we picked up from the gossipy old principal of Pusey at Oxford.

What could I ever have reported to you, Marigold, old dutchie, to whom life bound me with countless delicate threads, that late Sunday evening? What glowering glowing truth had been lobbed into our hearth? From that minute I knew two things: a shaft of joy as of steel and the very sharpness of that blade's isolation. My being was from that moment to be transfixed by a secret unshareable with you who shared my bed and table, a secret shareable only with her for whom prior love had turned as fatal as Paolo's for Francesca da Rimini … the Francesca who – look, my Lord! – *had not changed* in the essence of her since our union in the heat of our innocence: she was that same maiden bride. All these seventeen years of her motherhood she had carried her body's birth-secret without notion of sharing it with a soul, least of all him who made it. By her letting go of it to him with such insouciance, so unintendedly, her secret claim on him was spontaneously re-stated … as if to confront the Lord God himself with shoulders squared with *What has He ever got over us? The imprint of Love is in our son. That is the creative gift. There is no trumping it.*

Put my secret tears in your bottle, Lord. They are tears of joy.

Beloved wife, you now see face-to-face. No secrets hidden, all desires known. What could you have borne to hear?

Not that secret.

For an hour, Marigold, on my drive back to London, how I wept! At the wheel of my car on the M1 tears swept me in a gale. Through all that sunlit August sunset I wept, driving as if through the cloudburst drenching my face with the irreconcilability of my sorrow and my joy, sorrow and joy. This was my love-child, hermetic secret within me in our home. O the temptation to tell you what was there within me – to cast myself down before you in dramatic confession not of sin but joy in an orgy of truthfulness. The reality would have ripped you asunder and all we had made together!

'You look washed out, Simon … How was your Oxford friend? Girlfriend.'

I could swear I had never told you anything to warrant that correction …

How canny you always were, how mysteriously intuitive, on matters touching your mate's early manhood.

'Ah. Things move on. She's wedded to her Tory grandee. I told you.'

Would that I might consult my Lord … since He will know how something glinting there – gold chalice – had on the instant been recognised by her. God knows, joy is unexpungible.

A glass sheet had come down between us. Was it then at that instant the dementia began to creep upon you? – the vitreous seeping into the synapses of the mind, not perceptible yet ineluctable to distance you from what we, the rest of us, take as reality? Was it then? Was it *then*?

Returning to you that evening 'washed out', I went to bed early and dreamed. I had returned from a strange faraway voyage of several years' duration, carried in the bowels of an ocean-going ship that had sailed a vast distance to pagan and fearful shores. You, Marigold, were on the quayside to welcome me. The twins were with you – in my dream they were young, at three or four – and there you stood between them on the quay as I emerged out of the belly of the ship into the warmth of the English sunshine. How fresh you were and anxiously bright in a printed frock. As I was by way of stepping over the gunwales of the boat I held out my hands for you to catch my fingers and lean back to take the weight of me. Indeed you so attempted, but you failed.

You were too weak, and were dismayed at yourself for being so weak. And at that moment I saw, beneath that printed frock, how thin you had gotten in my long absence, pathetically *maigre*, wasted, which you would not have had me observe: yet it was so. I was pierced with sorrow, that same sorrow which had me weeping in my car.

You were as bone-thin my poor darling, in my dream, as you were to become in the last months of your dementia, unwilling to rouse your appetite and go on with what was left of you.

IX

Suddenly in this steep gully there is a thing live at my feet: a violent scurrying and bursting forth from a thicket here. And a savage pungency.

I am unalarmed: I am the alarmer. I am whipped back to Africa, to the equatorial forest by night, to Ituri. I have blundered upon the *couchement* of a boar in its refuge from the storm, immediately here: the very heat of the beast is evident to me – blundering into a densely wooded couloir, thicketed and jumbled with unexpected obstacles, *saggero, ardra*.

I know to draw upon the wisdom of forest beasts. If this was the *sanglier's* refuge, may it now be mine? This is as much my forest as the beast's. Now it is for me to find a hide to curl up in, to be banked around, to gather leaves to cover me, attempt sleep. And more: if the beast was here it will have water somewhere within scuttling range.

So indeed by my reading of its scent I have now found its nesting warmth, here in the hollow where the beast has been lying up! My body tells me that one side of this *couchement* is not natural rock but a rock wall made by man. It rises out of this steep earth by three or four feet in primitive slabs.

Here am I amid the ruined evidence of ancient man, primal dwellers of this foreign massif.

Here I can crawl away into my own non-being and have the storm thrash and shriek above me. Here I can be nothing. This is a sunken place. Slumped here into the sink-hole between the foot of the wall and jostle of weeds and saplings in the creature's stench, I feel guilty at its expulsion. Would that I shared it with you, O you sow who know not that God is Love, who need no God to teach you to die for your farrow. You are better than I, I who would fain fill my belly with the husks that you would eat and drink from that forest sump you slake at. I would have you share this *couchement* as I already share the warmth and odour you have left here, in this hollow primal man here has left for us. At that rim of my pygmies' forest where the great river snakes north to Lake Albert, my hunters and I once chanced on the site of recent battle between a giant forest hog and a lion. O giant tusked hog, how you fought to your death for your sow's farrow: there was your carcase, half-consumed, thrust deep into a thicket. That lion fought the duel of its life, such was the surrounding devastation. Such was love. Even the Bambuti stood in awe.

In my forest here, the predator here is Man. I am man, yet no predator.

I admire you, musty hog.

Here in utter blackness, I make my little pit by gloving my body in the dumb earth against the rock slabs. It is as proper for me as a neat grave. Who's to say it was not a mausoleum for those remnant Maures, black-a-maures, pre-Christian, pre-civilisation Africans, stranded on the wrong side when water of the melting northern ice divided continents. I take you to my heart like my Bambuti. Like them you are fortressed by your forest where you delved, hunted and nursed your fire, living out your lives in the dark and half-dark and leaving your bones. I am one with you, ancient men. Those Var peasants won't get us here, those who penetrate our forest massif only to shoot out all that breathes and scuttles, drag it forth, gut, skin and roast it; feast on it and get drunk. They know nothing of the beast's intimacies, its rootlings, fur and faeces. They'll soon be manning the search parties that you, Clare, will have initiated.

How I am comforted! – back among my beloved brethren whose forest is their all, sacred and benign, by which and in which and for which they have their being and go to their eternal rest.

They'll never find me here! Even if they bring dogs, the dogs' noses will be deceived by the scent of the *sanglier* whose hide is my hide and body-musk my musk. They will never find us here, me and my Maures and my swine. Let me live and die here with my forest moors. We'll share our forest with all the other creatures like my elfin pygmies in their bark from the *omutoma* tree, at work with arrows, pit-traps, nets and bamboo gins. When these cork-oaks grow old and die and drop or shed their limbs there's grub aplenty between bark and trunk, a thousand creatures with ten thousand legs to keep us fed. There are fungi, roots, sweet stems and berries. The forest is our father and our protector.

They'll never find us here, you remarked to me, Marigold, shy and alarmed, in that clearing where the Bambuti had admitted us in the Ituri forest. We had trekked out from Bubandi on the Lamia river with Samueli and fellow Mwamba porter, who warily despised pygmies as surely our Provençal bronze-agers warily once despised what remained of the Neolithic Maures. This was my fourth entry in and among my Bambuti, into their transient grove, and your first and only, Marigold. I carried Christian artefacts for the unlettered: Virgin and Child in porcelain, the Son of God twisted on the geometric cross carved out of teak. The missionary Simon Peter was in his evangelistic arc to arm them for another innocence.

Here they were in a half circle, folk I knew, each by name, elves draped or skirted in bark and velvet-monkey skins (but one in jeans), some with bows, some crouched, some standing, their lips half-open and their eyes wide in speechless awe. None moved. None had ever laid eyes on a white woman. I knew what they were thinking – that this was an intrusion too much; these four of us. Samueli was of their acquaintance from his childhood when his father traded with them, and had their lingo well enough; yet they did not rate him a proper person nor a person who read the forest by living it and winning its trust. Samueli was a *nyama,* creature, as they spoke him when I was alone with them: a less-than-human species like the rest of the Bantu villagers they encountered. Their obeisance to Samueli and his fellows was pretence.

I greet old Moke and he, the wit, responds, 'Here is the Long One with his lady and if he takes her hunting she will get trapped by the forest. The leopard will eat her.' This has them instantly falling about.

Amid the laughter, Marigold, you are glancing at me half-challenging, half in pity – maybe in anguish that I might awake to the delusion of my faith. It is because you love me and would not have me fooled. Your eyes saying What is it you can bring to these people? What can they have need of from you? Were they not all Christ's children before Jesus arrived to speak of children? – Are they not his children yet?

The texts thunder my head. '*"Suffer little children, and forbid them not, to come unto me, for such is the Kingdom of Heaven". And taking a child*' – it is Matthew reporting – '*he set him in the midst of them. Whosoever shall receive one of such children in my name, receiveth me. And whosoever shall not receive the Kingdom of Heaven as a little child shall in no wise enter therein.*'

Your unspoken protest, your darting plea, is What can you truly bring to them? They can't have any use for your message of suffering, of sacrifice, of redemption. They were designed to live in their own kind of darkness. Perhaps of God, if you insist.

Marigold, you were ready to parrot to me what I had brought back from my last long sojourn with my Bambuti and you had watched my own dilemma closing upon my head. You had watched me dragged into my own Christian crisis, using my terminology, not yours: on the challenge to intrude the G-word into his forest where G already *was* the forest, the provider, the protector, the master. They lived life whole, hence holy, in harmony one with another, knowing error but no evil, no sin, harbouring no resentment, no hate, no vengeance, being whole in the manner my Faith admired and Jesus preached yet which must elude all us non-forest dwellers. *What need do they have of it?* you once asked, meaning that terrifying sacrifice of God as Man by the cruellest method of execution men could devise … for the expiation of His fellows' vanity. Had I not the simulacrum of that climactic horror each three inches long as mementoes of the infinitely superior wisdom I had come to bring them?

'Your *metaphor*,' she flings at me like a steel dart.

And you my Bambuti knew nothing of vanity! No knowledge of it! You lived with and for one another with scarcely a quarrel, so quick to forgive, to heal any hurt by the balm of the group with no pointing of blame, since you were possessive of nothing – not territory, not goods, not chattels, not meat, not leaf shelters, not even mating partners. Every mother acknowledged the infant she had given birth to and the one who had caused her to conceive, yet every adult in the camp was mother and father to every child, and every oldie granny or grandpa.

The Bantu in the villages were stalked and nailed by the evil eye. They were beset by malign spirits and sorcery. Here sickness was no punishment; it was the way life was. Death was but the forest reclaiming its own. Thus they are children – I ventured to put it to you, Marigold – fit for the Kingdom.

You countered, Was I to be first to introduce them to hatred, fear and greed, that they might learn of Christian redemption? What did I need to save them from? Was mine a better innocence than that which I had been at such pains to take from them?

What you had perceived, Marigold, was my mission becoming reversed – that they were half-way to converting me. They were the very children Jesus spoke of, suffered to come unto him.

I in my churched role had no means of handling this dilemma, that to know Christ they must be weaned of their childhood into adulthood, the grime and greed of it, before they must wilfully re-learn it by the whip and ligature of the Faith. You saw my recognition of my soul's futility, how here I had arrived at my own beginning, how for my own sake I must confess it, how they were lilies of the field or birds of the air which neither spin nor toil.

So be it! For here was that spirit of joy that had fired my vocation to come to the forests of equatoria. What these Bambuti were still living was a primality of fragile but critical preciousness for man the sophisticate. They lived life whole in a manner that could not but elude the rest of us, yet which Jesus preached for such as us. Theirs was the only world they knew and supposed there was. *I* knew of the perilous vulnerability of their world, at the brink of their extermination. This was the last hour of this very remnant in the wide earth of gatherers and hunters and of the innocence Man had elsewhere grown beyond long long ago.

Neither of us yet had knowledge of the cave, Marigold. We arrived with no expectation of it. You were here because you pleaded not to be left alone with your bereavement among the ladies of the diocese, fervent for Jesus and their incessant good works. Yet also you would not have me crack in isolation beneath the dilemma you knew to be confounding me: that none can *become* like children except by the way of knowledge of good and evil. You loved me in my induced confusion, yet helplessly. If things were coming to a head between us, our path and purpose, hurtling to a crisis, it should be beyond the sight of the diocesan community, beyond any human eye capable of prying. Instinctively you had seized upon the forest. And that very night was to be the cave, and the cave's *molimo*.

From the start, you had glimpsed the spectre of inherent paradox at my first exposition of my intent, at Holy Trinity, Prince Albert Road – of bringing the gospel of innocence to the innocent. The world of corruption was indeed closing upon them, with pirate-logging on the Congo side of the frontier and game parks and tourism on the Uganda side. All that they knew of creation was menaced by extinction and their way of life with it. I might talk of a Christ-bound casket for their own purity, such as my Church endorsed. Now we each knew that to be fantasy. Their destiny was to be corralled, and alcohol and syphilis and a freakshow for visitors, enslaved by touristic tips for waggling their backsides in grass skirts. Was all this not what the Christian world had brought upon them?

'Your light will blind them,' you once came back at me.

'They'll not escape the light of day,' I countered.

'Light in whatever form. Literacy. Catechisms. The hostile sun.'

You saw me barging into Eden, making Innocence guilt. You would protect me from the consequences of my vocation, the absurdity of pygmies in their primal innocence slipping across into the innocence of Jesus of Nazareth's little children; without the baggage of its doctrine, without the redemption of the world by the son of that which I named God. Were they not pre-God (by any language), being pre-conscious, pre-I, as once were Eve and her consort when in their garden they did not know that they were naked?

Samueli did. Samueli had come to Christian faith with joy at release from the evil eye by the power of the cross, but I had to scold him on my second visit for exposing on the sudden to my Bambuti the painted wooden crucifixes the diocese had provided. The red paint of blood was visible on the hands and feet and pierced side. It was not apt. It was alarming. It had been part of my reason for sending Samueli back to Bundibughyo, out of the forest, on my long sojourn with them.

On my own return, Marigold, you had been oddly silent, scarcely enquiring what I might have achieved. Whatever course I was following, you seem to have decided, I was on my own.

And now I was back among them with you, in such raw bereavement. That very death of Jasper bound us in grief. But it was an accusation of our presence here in equatoria.

You ask me what Moke had said to set off the gale of laughter. I tell you that such mockery of your alienness in their forest is the warmest mark of welcome. Aüsu instantly assured you he would defend you from leopards. 'Kingwana is our brother and you our sister,' he announces gripping your wrist with two hands. He leads you to the leaf shelter which I, Kingwana, the Tall, will occupy near the camp's log fire. Aüsu being closest to me of all this Bambuti group has placed himself in charge of me. He had allocated a space for Samueli, but on the edge of the clearing, beyond our circle of intimacy. There he will stay with his fellow Mwamba, our porter. The joy in Aüsu's eyes at my return is at once recognisable to you, Marigold.

I had told you of Aüsu. He was wearing a G-string and a flap of bark before and behind. He was as near a convert as I had yet achieved among the Bambuti because he and I conversed on equal terms, so equal indeed that that I had got to telling him that he was as near to converting me to the Bambuti way of life as I was to converting him to the good news of Jesus Christ. There was depth of intelligence between us, founded in the delight of our comradeship. Aüsu from the very first had been as curious about me and my world that was not forest as ever I had been about his. It was Aüsu who had taught me enough of his language for me to tell them of a world in which the grace and generosity of any forest was absent, yet in which people could be engaged in tasks other than seeking food and protecting themselves. I had put it to Aüsu as his wife gave birth to their son and first child the interrogative concept *why*. Why things are. Why his

son so precious and unique would survive while mine so precious
and unique had not. Why life had been given to any of us. Why the
forest, why its munificence. Why it was uniquely for Man to delve for
answers.

He was fired and flattered and the imagination had grabbed at
the abstract, as I burrowed for words of Love and Truth and Life.
Indeed he was exhilarated. There had been opened up to him an
entire landscape for him to explore, in the cause of enlightenment. I
too, Marigold, had been uplifted by my entry through Aüsu into the
pygmies' entire realm of the forest, a realm of its own possessed by
them and possessing them, which they had to themselves with an
indefatigable sense of propriety, tolerating no violation by any who
were not of it in awe and intimacy, by which every Bantu villager
was excluded and kept at a distance by a hundred secret devices of
jungle lore withheld, mystery, territorial evanescence and pretended
servility. Only when I had sent Samueli back to Bundibughyo across
the great river and out of the forest, with his catechisms and his box of
wooden crucifixes, did Aüsu allow me – alone – admittance, and my
own awakening to their being.

Returning now with you Marigold, and with Samueli in tow,
that awakening is suddenly in hazard and I, covertly, am sick with
fear. You are intensely engaged. The thorn's scratch on your forehead
makes evident your vulnerability and your potential ferocity, a
ferocity directed towards me and our would-be mission among these
Bambuti. You yourself have become a participant, affronting any sense
you could be persuaded of: you, a woman of schooled intellectuality
engaged in bringing white man's juju and fetishistic talismans to a
bunch of forest dwarves in bark cloth.

'I am both beneath your good sense, and also above it' I wish to tell
you, but dare not. 'The crude myth of crucifixion and what followed
is beneath you, but its meaning above you.' I see the parallel for the
dwarves themselves: they are, in their primality, simultaneously

beneath us intruding providers of the Christian passport to life beyond the forest, and above us in the transcendent implication of that primal innocence. 'I love these people, Marigold, and I love you.' So my head thunders.

But for such love to invest our being it is to rise no less from that which is primal and beneath as out of the immortal and above. The double dialectic racked me. Tired and wet and strained in that dark, minuscule clearing I see mission and marriage in grotesque entanglement. You are so mercurial, in scorn of my missionary intent yet wonder at my own encountered wonder. I had returned from my long Bambuti co-habitance, back to you in your bereaved isolation, with a veiled joyfulness. Yet now you can by your presence here obliterate all that I have touched and seen and been possessed by, all that vital respect that had grown between me and them, these children of God as revered John, beloved of Jesus, would have them known.

'It is not for you to tell them that they are naked,' you come back at me sharply.

'For heaven's sake, Marigold. This is not a Sunday school. You don't need to defend them from me.'

You are *distrait*, dangerously agitated, as if I am threatening them with conversion. Samueli's fellow Baamba, so you saw – planters and reapers, keepers of livestock – had known the shock of the white man's coming two generations earlier. White man's instant master-culture and his creator-deity put to flight their daemons, all but scattering their powers. Yet these pygmies' deity is quite other. It is beneficent and trusted. It is their own forest; the whole and that which is holy. Your holy husband in his mission role and with Christian propositions indeed has no right to challenge the meaning of all they know from birth and infinite inheritance. Even the Baamba, in scorn of Bambuti as diminutive and primal, sneakingly revered their forest-wisdom. That wisdom is their primordial link which sustained and protected them and gave their world its meaning. The forest folk are central Africa's first people. All the sites bear the numinous designations in the Bambuti vernacular, which I now haltingly speak. From the pygmies the Baamba buy root medicine and their drumwood, the dark tree-core, for its resonant authority ...

Our spat is evident to Samueli.

'Do not go with them into their cave,' he suddenly warns. I turn on him:

'Why, Samueli?'

'They seek to capture Jesus.'

'What do you mean?'

'They seek to capture him who once was dead and has come back from dead; to make him theirs. This is Jesus, who belongs to you. They seek to make you a *molimo-mbandua* and so catch Jesus.' He makes the catching movement.

So now there is this contrary fear in you, Samueli, that they are by way of converting me, beguiling me and my soul into pygmydom. That is what I seek, what I know I must risk, for the sake of my own truth and even for the sake of you, Marigold, tarring me with pagan innocence.

Oh Samueli, they will never take *you* to their cave. Your people are not forest people: your intrusion would desecrate it.

'You should leave Jesus behind,' Marigold says.

'Don't be concerned, darling. Jesus understands. He takes no orders from me. We are here to learn something from them.'

'What, then?'

'How to be one with creation. The untellable wisdom,' I quote ... *The animals, plants, men, hills, shining and flowing waters.*

All at once I am struck by the wisdom of the human body, that by this body we learn the loving of our God. So Aqivah, Rabbi supreme, spoke of the Song of Songs how *the whole universe was worth the day that book was given to Israel.*

Now you speak up.

'It is a mark of trust in you, Simon, that they would take you there. Moke and Aüsu and the others seek what they recognise as your gift, your capacity to learn. And mine. *I* shall go.'

My heart jumps at this sudden boldness, and you simultaneously frail. You are to catch them with your bow and the strings it serves and they to counter-catch you with bow and arrow and with drums and reeds. At the first dark growl of the *molimo* circling the camp there is wild light in you. 'Because they will not admit Samueli,' you persist, telling me what I know, 'he is afraid for us, and for your gospel. He has no right to be afraid. They do us honour. If they may not reach for you, however will you reach for them?'

Now you are drawing on me. The tables are turned. You have seen them read in you a fount of authority, they *heard* in your strings the authority of the invoking of music, and a responsiveness to the growls and the hoots of the *molimo* and the rattle of hidden *molimo* drumming that is beginning to infect the forest. Oh, Samueli!

So I set forth. Clutching my scripture book in its green covers I have had since Cuddesdon, I struggle for an inward space of detachment; I take on something of your godless father, Marigold, Hegelian sociologist, carapacing myself by observation, the conceit of academia looking out from the cloister of my improvised cosmogony, upon these forest dwarves, half my size and bulk and more-than-half in darkness: on Aüsu, Moke, Masisi, Kenge, Mahomo and their women who are once the guardians of the *molimo*; now dappled, flitting folk like you, ye Neolithic Maures among whom at last I have found my refuge, entering the earth's bowels for the wisdom of intimacy with pristine creation.

Was it for me, Bambuti – is it for me, Maures? – to come in among you with unassailable presumption that I carry with me a Truth you have no inkling of, in your ten thousand generations of forest gathering and hunting and loving?

How dare I?

Marigold, you read in me the alarm and caution as each of us stripped to the skin to don the smoky bark cloaks required for us by Aüsu and the women. You are the bold one, the venturesome, entering among those little people by that rock orifice into their underworld. Beside you Moke, wholly trusted, carries your violin in its case with reverence. He opens the case by the light of the fire: your music and authority like a Jesus-foetus in your surrogate womb, amid that circle of clapping women, grunting, *aye-yea-yea-aye, yea-aye-aye-yea*. Bare-chested now, you have put him to your chin and move with the thump of the drum and the stomp of rattles of mollusced metal on the ankles of the shunting of diminutive Humanity circling the fire, old and young alike entranced, with staring eyes and darting hands.

Somehow Marigold you have acquired an ankle-rattle. You are eerily pallid in the smoky firelight as if you were conjured by Aüsu the intoning leader, whose face of clay-smeared white your skin resembles. Your loosened hair is made Maenadic by the brilliance of your bowing and your eyes are closed, but Aüsu's head is orderly with its tonsured wig of dry grass and the civet pelt capping his skull. His neck is strung with pale shells. His skirt is also of bunched grass, held at his waist with a snakeskin, and his eyes are staring out all but blind from lids dyed red behind dark glasses. His hands too are red-dyed, each with its wooden rattle which he uses like a gavel to summon each shift of the discourse. What speech is this? It is their lingo of immemorial privacy that like the immemorial forest knows no tense but *now* and has no need of grammar more than prayer needs liturgy: naked language. All this possessing us with the savage rhythm, driving the bark-clad circle in their drum-obeisant strut.

Within that resonant and impenetrable dark, the constant growl of the bass bamboo.

Suddenly an unearthly diapason leaps forth as if out of the belly of the chamber: an Mbuti I had not noticed is crouched at the drumside blowing by a reed inserted into the belly of the drum. Out of his own belly and throat-roar comes an amplified voice no longer human or of recognisable human provenance. As Aüsu intones the women respond to him antiphonally, so that here's a rhythm laid upon a rhythm; and you Marigold have joined the antiphony, making your mesmeric *obbligato*. I, loosened at last by my gourd, have emerged from my cloister-site of observation to be snared and woven into the thread of spirit-song of Aüsu, its refrain ever in praise of the forest. For we ourselves – you and I – are the topic of it, we and the *geist* resurrection I first entered the forest to bestow them.

They have admitted us here for our endorsement of the transcendent truth-leaping death of the forest Jesus: the beat and invention of the drummer and the drum that he is one with, he who had elicited from your own violin seminal inspiration, across the soaring and searching lyric of the instrument and every expressive device of urgency by double and triple stopping, aërial harmonics bowed against the bridge, *spiccato* and *pizzicato, glissando* and *staccato,* the rasp and flutter of your making, and swaying; rump-alive and innocent. I am astonished.

They feed it you with their unconscious wonder. From the cavity of the Mittenwald at your chin there leaps the truth of your spirit, the kenotic gift of the fashioned wood: out of the fiddle's void and the void of the drum is the word uttered. This is your letting-go into creation's pagandom, Marigold, a little drunk and beyond exhaustion. Three-quarters naked you too among those buttock-decorated women stalk and flit, hunter and quarry, escaping (Aüsu tells) the wiles of the leopard Moke had conjured on your arrival and now guarded by the ever-vigilant forest. You astonish yourself.

Here was to be the generative source of your inward Threnody for Jasper: music at birth.

When after uncountable hours we emerged into the listening forest, there lay just visible the little heaps of our abandoned clothes, as if they were the droppings of visitant creatures that had no business here in this true forest-world, then had left their evidence and scuttled off. And *now* I repent, Marigold, without reserve; now that you are dead. Now I gently grieve. Such bigot as might have entered that cave has surrendered to this root-world, cave-place of the birth of music centred upon the drummer no bigger than his drum and slave to his genius and upon his squatting partner's roaring diapason – the frail firelit circle chants in antiphony, the growling bass bamboos and hidden *molimo* horn invoke all that is, seen and unseen.

What *you* have brought them, Marigold, has sealed them, my Bambuti, my Maures: a quicksilver glimpse by sound and shunting feet and darting hands of apocalyptic impulsion. You and I were forbidden to speak, were we not, of what transpired in our cave. *Tell the vision to no man,* it is written, *until the Son of Man is risen again from the dead.* How tightly mute were you on the tramp back to the forest clearing in fingers of first light. How my heart bled for you on that night tramp, knowing that such ascent must mean descent, a dreadful plummeting … I knowing and loving you.

Then by God you turned on me. You turned and railed that I should *dare* to trump their right to the forest wisdom bestowed on them as gift, love, reverence, and creative inspiration.

Squatting in the clearing by the embers of the fire, Samueli had been waiting for us in baleful turmoil as morning light was filtering in … He quoted at me darkly from Isaiah, *And the idols he shall utterly abolish, and they go into the holes of the rocks, and into the caves of the earth, for fear of the Lord!* he pointing with his finger at the passage he had found and seized upon that very night of our long absence in the cave, in the belly of the earth.

Samueli, you were never truly to recover your trust in me. I had crossed over to the enemy that night. I had supped with the Devil. I was blighted by the forest men's *nkisi.* O baleful Samueli. *She* had beguiled me and had me eat of the forbidden as if she were Eve. You expected no better from the mem, for you alone had come to note she eschewed any act of worship, had never seemingly laid before Our Lord even her grief at His taking baby Jasper. Hence, you supposed, she had persuaded me to defy and disobey and had led me into the pit.

There she will have let go – you could tell, Samueli: she and I in Bacchic purgation, beyond the reach of Jesus. There in self-violation she was violated, Samueli, was she not? while you cowered in your tent – and in nine months was your proof of it. The twins were born, one or other of them by fornication with the Devil that very cave-night. You have it, Samueli: that night was her conceptual night of music, penetration of generative semen which out of surrender makes art, conjugation which makes life, the flint's spark, scintilla, the orgasmic event that in its happening is gone.

Hence my Marigold, mem, came to compose her masterwork, Samueli, her threnody. Aüsu had peered up at me through the smoke and noise and ludicrous shades to tell me, amazed, This your lady is *mbandua,* witchery.

And you Marigold, ex-witch, back in the clearing, have turned upon me in furious injustice … that I could have presumed to stand aside in that cave's unpenetrated shadows to wrap myself in my God of Love. 'This was love,' you hissed; 'and resurrection. Life. His is the aboriginal myth, Simon. It is the same gigantic story! Don't they love their jungle? This is the Creator in his bounty. They are bursting with praise and thankfulness. They invoke his presence and speak with him and for him. *Dixit dominus.* They ask him to intercede when they are broken-hearted. Are you to confound them with your rules and rituals, and prelates and prayer books? Are you to drown their music in hymns? Jesus Christ knew nothing of the jungle. He went into the desert to hear the voice of God, they go into their cave, the belly of the Earth. What better myth have you to peddle them? They brought us in and disclosed their secrets … and you stand by watching and judging. How dare you, Simon!'

I am bludgeoned into silence. Never have I known such an

outburst. It is grotesquely unjust. For I am alongside you in my understanding. Your tears are unstoppered now. I bury my face in your shoulder as you retail all that I already know of your heart's dilemma. My understanding of you is useless. It is as if you have come to know these Bambuti more intimately in your first encounter than I in my five months of sharing in the forest their daily lives. And so it could be.

All at once your tongue breaks loose.

'What is theirs but the God of Love? There is no place for words. They need no words for trust in their spirit of this forest. It is their universe. They live their spirit. The bark! The clay! The drum. Aüsu's skins and grasses! They trust and share and thank for all that spirit's gifts and speak his voice, their *abanduas*! They *love* the spirit of their universe. They invoke his powers of healing. What else do *you* do? What better? They entreat the bounty of his creation and rejoice in it. Your Harvest Festival, Simon. They sanctify it all – what more do you want? They consign to him the souls of their dead. Even Jasper's soul. Aüsu sang of Jasper. You heard him. Who are you to deny them foreknowledge of a God of Love?'

My God, Marigold, what words you found.

'What do you purport to bring them with Palestinian myths? It's nothing more than an elaborated version of the same entry by man into the presence of God and the fleeting sharing of his voice.' The tears were shining.

I am fearful that Samueli overhears you and shall carry the report out … that the Devil had got you and challenged me and my God and struck me down.

So it had. The monumental futility reared up over me at my presence here among these people – this remnant humanity that could neither read nor write, whose only word for love was an utterance signifying union and who half-wordless were closer to their Creator than I could ever attain to. And they were the single pretext of my being in Africa where I had brought my bride and our first-born was sacrificed. A devilish stench chokes my gullet. Somehow you had got hold of the cardboard box of miniature wooden crucifixes which Samueli had insisted on bringing back with us, and somehow you had pushed that box into the embers of the compound fire beside us, and the acrid smoke of the smouldering paint was reaching me.

It had begun to rain. Great drops from the canopy infinitely above hissed on the embers of Samueli's fire. The futility of my life's endeavour and my marriage had become one and the same and were spoken to me here in this jungle compound's darkness at a site which no other man or woman who had ever cared about me could possibly locate. In such bottomless irresolution I wish to kneel and pray. Marigold the non-believer was speaking here for me who had presumed to bring the word of God in faith to a people of prior innocence, that very innocence Jesus Christ enjoined as his premise for entry into the Kingdom. She had been inspired by that same Aüsu in the civet cap and ankle-rattles and shades that surely rendered him all but sightless in the smoke of the cave, improvising in his fragmentary verses from the resurrection story I had embedded here in previous months when she was grieving our son.

Was it not now for me to re-wind the entire narrative of man's recognition of the power of love that brought man into being? – I to re-wind to nothing, other than this minuscule forest remnant of pristine forest dwarves, who will have vanished from the earth in fifty years?

Oh, I had arrived at where I had begun – at where this phylum of the human race had begun: at that point of self-recognition where such recognition sought only to escape its attainment, by its chosen, desperate act of love.

For where had we got to, since our race of creatures were all gatherers and hunters?

Augustine wrote, *All scripture is vain*, because He is known only beyond language. Here in utter darkness and utter silence, in a place untraceable by the rest of man, in the nullity of endeavour and the irrelevance of purpose, shall my God declare himself to his creature whom he made unique by the gift to speak His name, yet who must abandon all his powers of speech if his Word is to be heard?

What if we in all the universe of your creation, Lord, your thing *Man* was not present here, not so much as a vagrant, forest-lost, upon the sedimentary surface of the provincial planet Earth, to gather and hunt and seek Your face? How impossibly slender is this human thread, this remnant that alone can say *God*, say 'Lord', give thanks? The fire at my feet is gone; the forest and its utter darkness are without limit.

Where are you of the prior innocence, my Bambuti, without whom I could not survive a week?

What, God, could You have done without these children of innocence all these aeons of pre-history?

Oh Marigold, my Marigold, who had entered in among them and won admission by your bow with its resounding void! When the pygmy daemon force had silenced me and the entire forest, and you and I—in shock – dismantled anew, took to our sleeping bag, with what abandon did you possess me, what savage joy!

Indeed, Samueli could never be the same thereafter. No less could I. The twins' birth confirmed the sacrilegious betrayal such as Samueli presumed. To the Mwamba Samueli what else was one or other of those twins but the Dark One's semination? Yet our Bambuti, when they were to hear of your double birth rejoiced for us, Marigold, praising the forest and giving me a new name. For them it was they who had opened up your womb and made good the gift of new life. Thenceforward I was Father of the Cave Twins. I knew that if I had entered primal Africa for any purpose at all it was to submit not preach, learn rather than to teach, and offer back to them whatever doctrine I arrived with, as two babbas wrapped in bark-cloth.

O you ancient Maures of this cleft rock cleft of mine and yours where you've admitted me. You accept me, don't you, now that I am shriven? – you, and my Bambuti, my primal people. And *now* at last, here's my Marigold. I hear your voice. *They are the forest priesthood, Simon, these emulima-abandua, Aüsu, Moke, and the others. They interpret the forest's spirit, they sing with its voice just like the singer of the Song of Songs.*

You see the tears on *me*.

I am drowsy here, and fuddled beneath the storm. I hear the sacred song, *Catch us the foxes, the little foxes…* the ancient scripture of spoken love *Oh my dove, that art in the clefts of the rock and in the secret place.*

And it is there in the depths of the forest, so we each knew, that our twins *are* conceived – in a sleeping bag you have wriggled into for the security of it at the fingers of first light under the *mongonzo* leaves, whether or not you have set yourself against conceiving again. You love me: without me would not wish to live, I hear again you telling me. Anything more there might be to say can be truly said in music only, music which renders words redundant …

Are you now to allow me sleep, Marigold? And while I sleep, unfound and unfindable, condone? – you who in life here disallowed yourself a life hereafter?

Was it indeed I who made memory take leave of you? who touched the switch of your affliction?

Was it I?

X

For how many years had I not seen you Evie, nor had knowledge of you beyond what Clare gratuitously had dropped at our occasional encounters? Then the Church of England in its jumbled wisdom elevated me to my Cheltenham bishopric and you, Evie, hearing of it, wrote to me by hand from Stourton Bassett, *Dear Simon*, a plain statutory Dear. *Victor joins me in congratulating you on being made a bishop. Whatever will they think of next! – No, but I'm serious, and most impressed. As you probably already know, Victor is a Church Commissioner. With love from Evie. PS I enclose a picture taken just the other day with our Gyles*: and there was a glossy coloured print, quite small, of you and Gyles, aged twenty-three or so, posing each with a racket, and a tennis net behind. There was no cause to show the picture to anyone else, nor the little note that accompanied it.

It was many months later, tidying my middle tray in the study of our suffragan's residence, that I chanced upon the letter in its original envelope and with the photograph inside.

On my turning it over, blood ran cold.

I read on the back of the envelope and in your pencilled hand, Marigold,

how proud your son would be if he could know

Unsigned. Quite faint. Subjunctive. Unpunctuated. Awaiting my eyes, whenever, if ever.

When had you pencilled those fell words, Marigold? The letter had been around for the better part of a year.

And how did you come to write such words? Evie had so conclusively assured me in her garden, *Only me. Now you.*

What on earth could have prompted, that faint pencilling? How could anything have leaked? By what instinct or intuition?

The thought of Clare leapt into me, – that in years long past Evie may have let slip something about the prompt arrival of an heir for Victor, her 'honeymoon conception', perhaps by some glancing hint from Evie with a narrow look, binding Clare to a secrecy less than devout, or else a spoken pact of confidence whose rigour time could have corroded.

I am in a cold sweat. Look at the wording of Evie's letter – *our Gyles.* Yet how else in just such a reference to herself and Victor would she have dashed off a spontaneous note?

The deduction your message carries, Marigold, is so lapidary, so implacable – the faint pencil, addressed to none, no date, no initial. It is as if my companion-spouse, bonded by vow, mother of our children, co-tolerator of all that a life together daily brings, has entered Evie's letter like a sleepwalker and as to a sleepwalker there has been revealed an ancient secret of such devastation that your hand, in sleep, has required me to be confronted by its exposure.

Then I see it. I have glanced back at the photograph of the two figures standing by that tennis net. There is the woman, *ecce mulier,* gazing into the camera's lens with a pent vitality, as if the eyes were speaking to a certain other … while the young man alongside her is – *is I* at that very age: at that instant of the lens' blink, unmistakably *I* in early manhood, on the cusp of university and real life, Francesca's Paolo at the weaning. *That* is what on the instant you saw, Marigold. Inescapably *yes*, and at the same instant reading all else: the latent love, sleeping Eros, sleeping lord, whose rapture's flame had not after all been extinguished. And reading how she, Evie, who on sight of the way the camera (most likely held by Victor) has caught the young man, could not bear to deny the boy's blood-father sight of it too.

What could I now do, Marigold, for you at the revelation of such a rapier wound – you who had loved me with your heart and your strength and the soul you'll not admit to? You had sleepwalked into this, and in the daze of half-unawakened nightmare had pencilled your ciphered message, a whispered *Miserere*, a melisma emitted to the sky by a shepherd on a high rock half-blinded by his sorrow.

What action was open to me, in whom you had placed your life in trust, for whom you had hazarded your talents? A blundering confrontation? A searing exposition, a zigzag analytical narrative? *–oh yes, darling, this haply occurred* (These things happen), *at that age, in that concatenation, on the lip of being ordained and a solemn vow of chasteness.* Oh!

What would be left of us and ours among the debris of explaining?

So I never saw that piercing note of yours. Into the drawer that smelled of sandalwood with the rest of 'Private Correspondence' went the letter and the photo and the unread version, in the original envelope.

I did pray, Marigold. I spoke to none but God. I prayed.

I prayed the boy, my son, this living soul in thankfulness. How could I else? And prayed his mother – her willed hazard with the pill. How could I else?

I prayed our daughters born in their sac of substitution for that brother they could never know who were now subtly and secretly embrothered, the daughters nonetheless informed by what was never spoken, an epiphatic gnosis, fearful of encountering their father in the nudity of his superstition which saw them born orphaned of their sibling. In his cathedral sermon at the Christening Bishop Kule named them Anthea and Oonagh *Mukirane*, given to a baby born following a sibling that had died. Thus they had grown, perpetually assuaging the remorse of their mama whose secret burdens they read and read beyond not only my vision but her very own perception.

Thus also it was, within weeks of that discovery of mine, that the twins came to me each from their distant homes with what they had begun to observe in you: those odd lacunae in memory. It was Oonagh first who mentioned, on the phone from Australia, that on her fortnightly calls by phone you seemed quite to have forgotten what had been talked about at length on the previous call. Then Anthea at her East Anglian University remarked similar lapses. 'I think Mum isn't making perfect sense, and isn't aware of it.' Then all at once a cluster of recent confusions and petty absences of mind – teaching appointments overlooked, gloves left behind, her car abandoned at a pupil's home while she came home by bus. Marigold was assuming a disquieting shape, a stranger in the room not precisely noticed hitherto, unpredictable, with an occlusion of recall that might have been haphazard or somehow devised to put away, out of reach, suspicion of life-long, love-long duplicity. Could this be a willed confiscation of memory that might come to corrode the entirety of you Marigold?

Marigold?

I phone Oonagh and hear her tell me what she, as a student of Public Health, knows of dementia, its manifestations and symptoms. I cut in to ask whether her Ma had spoken of any shock, a hidden grief …

'What do you mean, Dad? Hidden from you?'

'Oh, Oonagh *mambusia*. You know how she can let things secretly gnaw at her ... ' Oonagh was the closer to you by virtue of living at such a distance.

'I sometimes feel, Dad,' she said, 'you don't know where Mum is coming from.' In the gender-jargon of the day they presumed to lay their parents on the dissecting table. Such was adulthood. The love of God had no workable meaning for either twin. And Anthea was to ask me – Anthea, for whom Africa was ever my own self-serving aberration: *Do you never imagine, Dad, that Mum could will forgetting?*

Would to God, now, I am permitted to enter that pristine nothingness, of being without selfhood, such dispossession as I had dared aspire to as an ordinand years ago in the discipline of my retreat. That was the very citadel of spirit which I had permitted Evie to storm in spontaneous innocence.

What man of God am I? Am I now to regain it? Here in this hog-hole, against the breccia left by this massif's last true inhabitants, forgotten Moors marooned on European soil? I am their revenant priest of the order of Melchizedek, hunkered and cowering from the shrieking storm.

Would to God I am permitted to enter that pristine nothingness, the vital polarity whereby loss of life – of memory, will and senses – is the price of saving it. Would to God I am admitted to the nullity of that pearl of verse

Where there is nothing, there is God. The Word
Came to my mind, it might have been a flower
Dropt from a rainbow.

May that nullity lie in wait with love resembling the fisherman's hook that was the perception of my *Meister*. Once the hook is taken, God is sure of his catch, twist or turn as it may.

Nothing brings a man closer to God than the sweet bond of love.

He whom this hook has caught is caught so fast that foot and hand, mouth, eyes and heart and all that is his, belong only to God.

If it should be that a man and a woman have accepted love for one another, how will *that* love be sustainable and inviolable? How shall it not be spent, evanescent, substantively nil? Its truth, Evie, forming and in-forming us on our quitting childhood, is to alloy like bronze the gift of its invention in the ancient fire which is God's love.

Ah. Let me sleep in this hoghole, sleep on to awake into another world where all these things are comprehended and condoned and raised to that plane where one love does not annul any other but is the equal medium. We hear of heaven. We and Jesus speak of life eternal.

There is no case to plead, nor cause. There is no case but that very condition of Man which men cannot but attribute to you, Lord, and no cause but that single Love which cannot but flow from you, Creator.

We in our hides and burrows, our murked crevices, in the depths of any forest and the night, beneath the rage of any storm, shall love the Lord our God with all our mind and heart and strength, and shall love each other of flesh and bone and blood as our selves. That love is One, Heaven knows. We your creature by this fluke of knowing who we are, know of our isolation and encircling death, and so know also you, Lord: You enter revealed upon the plane where you preside, sharing with us your loving presence. That happened and was witnessed and believed. God knows, they died for it as had You in Jesus. Your cowering creature of this very day cannot but claim uniqueness, grasped and sustained by Love which uniquely and for ever and ever is total, holy, without limit or qualification.

As with you, Lord, so with creature. Any person worthy of the embrace of Love is sacred too. This love we speak is One-for-One, each rising to the other with the reciprocated urgency of joy in abandonment of self. If ever a man sees himself as One, or a woman likewise, he or she Loves One other. We are not God, yet indeed are in Your image. If we love any other we love as God loves us.

Merciful God, the act of love which generates your species Man endorses that uniqueness. You endorse this act. Wherever and however Man's uniqueness is violated, Lord, the flesh of Your making is at odds with the spirit, a violation least expungible.

Yea, Lord, it pleads redemption. The least betrayal of human love forfeits the right to share the presence of Your Divinity, the singleness of Your love.

Lord, have mercy.

Let me now find oblivion here, beneath this storm.

Christ have mercy. If the first gift of Your love is life, the next is death.

By your mercy, recognise me in my readiness to be gone to You.

XI

I have awoken upon the entire and perfect stillness of a forest dawn …
Pale dawnlight strikes the underside of the sweet chestnut canopy
high above my head in this steep flanked gully. In a disorder of dark
rocks and vegetation I am cramped and cold and thirsty. My dream
as yet unfinished is of this very forest rallied to my cause, the horde
of trees mobilized and marching as to war with me and for me, their
distinguished commander, with the ark of their covenant, yet the trees
nobler than man and woman in their withstanding of the storm, in the
grandeur of their reaching for the light, and in their marching and singing
and unfurling of banners of their branches, breaking the skyline with
pennants and paeans in certitude of victory. We are to conquer together
the topmost heights of the world to establish new peace upon it.

By means of my dreaming and of being dreamt, the forest has
evaluated me and initiated me into its company of members, which

are its creatures and trees and and their saplings and all the vibrant *kinder* of its *garten*. I am admitted now by consent of its inner council into its lit glades and dark gulches and beneath its ever-spreading canopies – admitted, known and welcomed. All these components rejoice for and with me. At their behest I have inherited the forest mantle of my human predecessors here, who are numbered among us sometimes as trees but also as miniature people. The Bambuti of my old companionship are, in my dream, here among us, unexpectedly and with a frisson of shock perceptible: Aüsu, Moke, all the others, stock still at the entrance to a glade, played upon by dappled light and shadow as am I also, in green shirt and russet trousers cramped into this hollow … played upon by dappled dawnlight.

All of us *forestiers* have adopted the slogan *THE WAY OUT IS IN*: we take up this cry and we brim with love for one another and for the commanding Hand by which we are accorded our eternal being. Yet, in my dream, I who am their latest initiate, am of secret and unique significance for the entire forest as the articulator of their truth for each one of them, indeed, and together. This secret significance, in my dream, has placed on me now, on my waking, a secret and undying obligation of allegiance and of speech.

Holy, holy, holy. Sabaoth forest Lord.

Let all that hath breath, praise you Lord.

Black-backed beetle, you are my small sabreur, busy in your corner amid the leaf mould of your kingdom. How kingly you render black on the backplate of your cuirass to celebrate this sunshaft filtered privately and horizontally to you and me. What transfiguration is this, scarab? With this primavera rising out of creation's waters, from your blackness you have made indigo, cobalt, cerulean, sapphire blue and the green of every ocean in the world, you are the vitreous invention of a thousand eyes, expectant for recognition. You slept the storm out. You are oblivious now of nothing but the dazzling darkness of your joyful being.

All is utterly silent. Beetle, nothing moves but your six legs, your quivering antenna, as you ease your way up this green stalk and are now in active contemplation of a transom stem, a crucifix which in silent metaphor pierces the universe with the crux of nullity and all that is, Seen and Unseen.

Silence peals the thunder – who told me that?

Absence experienced proclaims the presence.

My cavity here is where the boar was. Even now I scent the comfort of it. I can see where it has foraged and broken twigs. If there were husks here it rejected, I would eat them. Soon I will extricate myself and follow its track down to where there's a waterhole. There I will lap the pigs' mud and slime. I am reduced to nothing. So I rejoice. Even my reputation has been trampled into the mud: I'll be laughed to scorn. I am impervious to shame. I have attained to *nothing*!

All you good friends, besieged in Colin's villa, have been outflanked by me here in this wood in secret. You in your elegant villa; every one of your guests, Clare, and you yourself, surrogate of your absent son, have been trumped by the true prodigal. I have been brought poverty that I may know riches.

He who feeds on death, that feeds on men, possesses life supereminently. This 'metaphysical mystery' of William James that I quote to my Oxford students is the mystery that meets the secret demands of the universe. It is the truth of which the true ascetic has been the faithful champion. Listen on, my pupils in the class of life. 'The folly of the cross, so inexplicable by the intellect, has, yet, its indestructible, vital meaning.' And the naturalistic optimism of wealth-makers, economic planners, aid distributors, benefit dispensers, elective politicians of every hue, is 'mere syllabub and sponge cake'.

Beetle, you and I know that.

Whatever primal man was here in this ravine in this forest of this vast massif, learned that. He toiled in mines and scraped out pits for the ore of reddened earth and streaked rock with which his ancestors dyed the bones of their dead. Maybe these faced slabs which rise to a pygmy's height out of the roots and saplings to make a windowless wall now ruined, were slabs for your primal smelter.

You are gone and it was vain. You are all but blotted out from the book of life as utterly as these my Maures who too were children of the forest, rootling and hunting, trusting their forest as we of the faith trust our Maker, glad of its bounty, in harmony, in reverence, as utter children, children to this same god I have been schooled in, these five or ten millennia since our forest days. I am one with you now and have lived among you for ever and have loved you for ever, naming this Love. So you Maures, so you Bambuti, thus contained, shall have outlived all those others who have come and gone, those men of moment, fame and money and flashes of power for whom the forest is unknown to their world of getting and spending yet of all that is, what we see and cannot see, begotten not made, and of one substance with Him by whom all things are made. Here is my nothingness. I am of you by my love and for you, my fellows, *mes frères*.

My Bambuti, you and I know that it was vain and not vain. The gift of life the forest gave you could not be refused. My vocation to be with you could not be declined. All was vain and all was likewise holy. God of mystery and indefinability be praised. God be praised, Father, Holy Ghost and Son. I have had no function among you except to interpret your darkness for an ignorant world and find in your deep forest gloom and pitchy cave a source not of dark but of light; find in what pain you knew and sorrow and evanescence of life the concomitant of eternal joy; find in acceptance of death the *sine qua non* of life; find in weakness the first criterion of strength; find from strife and stress the sweet converse of peace; find in being marooned in the last of the pristine forest your ground of love and holy trust. You would say, Death is a 'big thing; it is of the forest', which is the guardian of Life.

You give me my release by the last embers of the nightly logs that our six *mongongo*-leaf shelters encircle beneath the canopy of mighty trees. You were locked into the treedom like Ariel, and I would free you from the outside world of enslavement to booze and beggardom at Bubandi, jigging asses for the tourist lens, weaving from forest stems purposeless trippers' trinkets, corralled by Game Wardens bearing guns, demeaned, degraded, violated by schooling and raped by religion. God forbid, my beloved charges of the forest, you of raw creation, of the divine whole, of that which is One, of the bed of language. I pray to God to spare you preachers who deny your home Truth they know nothing of.

Out of that One let there issue from your throats and musical artefacts sounds of infinite primality, warnings of leopards, greetings, homing signals, appeals for help, pleas of need, coos of content, of mutual recognition; whoops of the chase, 'vocalise', as once you said, Marigold, and out of vocalise the first person singular – I, then Thou. You, my Bambuti, from ancient times took on the lingo of whichever Bantu tribe settled nearest to you, to cultivate with hoes (possessing iron) half as big again as you, to whom you were linked by barter, medicine, bushmeat and music. You feigned obeisance for those Baamba of the mountain foothills, yet you were always fortressed by your own domain, your magnificent sanctuary, your forest which they feared. You cast for them the stem-fluted *erirenga*, you brought them boles of the *omwamba*, from secret places, as yet unhewn, for the hollowed-out communion of the drum. Those Baamba would confide to me that you Bambuti still had your own language but so secretly that you would not permit another ear to hear it or even know of it.

Performing with them on the reed-flute, Marigold, you yourself overheard Aüsu and his fellows exchange the gutturals of that pre-speech of theirs such as is never uttered but in intimate collaboration as when working upon the *omwamba* bole to extract by bellowsed fire the sacred resonance of that dark secret wood. We jointly, Marigold, were intruders upon the intensity of the *ngoma*-maker's craft, fashioning exquisite resonance, spellbinding those children with sound that preceded speech and superseded it. The drum-sound was the Word *sans* words, as in the manner and authority of the kiss of love that silences speech with communication far sublimer, infinitely sublime. For that non-speech you and I shall ever vouch, Evie. What you and I thus know, we know.

All scripture is vain, saith Augustine.

Let us be as little children, as pygmies.

You, pygmy *ngoma*-maker, Masalito, worked to make the perfect emptiness, first with a gouge of metal got from the Baamba out of the metal-yielding Ruwenzoris, and finishing it by red embers and hot stones churned in the sacred cavity to harden yet further the wood and smooth its inner belly. You click and turn to your sister's son-child apprenticed to you, to guide and approve. Only the pygmy hand is small enough, and the strong arm slim enough, to enter the collar of that cavity to work it. In ancient days, so you revealed to me, before the proximity of Bantu, when there were no others than those who lived and died by gathering and hunting, you made the drum's hollow by fire alone.

You would live here contentedly, my Bambuti, proto-Moors of Africa, in this very forest-massif of my present entrapment You would never have hunted the forest out, you would have revered its treasures. So in Ituri you stripped the *omutoma* for no more than the bark you need to keep you warm and sling your papooses. On my massif here the natives strip the bark for gain, for industry.

Before my eyes, where I am crouched to lap at the waterhole I have tracked to, a rotten cork-oak has fallen to the forest floor, just such a toppling as you Bambuti would instantly be delving for its teeming source of nourishment: a city of clandestine life and privacy entire in itself between trunk and loosened bark, dank and dark, a teeming community of grubs, mites, tribes of woodlice, centipedes and millipedes, ants upon excursions, pupae, larvae, myriad eggs, slugs asleep each of its own beauty in the streaked and swirling beauty of its own world of fallen and decaying tree … My black beetle was an envoy to this inner universe of beauty, as gratuitously bountiful of hue and flow as a woman's hair unpinned.

Everywhere is resurrection, look! – out of what has died, this treasure-house. I praise you, Jesus. Amid the bounty and fellowship and beauty and grace I give thanks for what has overflowed in creation to its overflowing. Look how the beetle has outlived the storm and how it is so intent and full of wonder climbing stems and exploring the underside of leaves, their veined beauty as exquisite as the wings of angels, and having discovered hastens on to repossess as heir the inheritance of the entirety all that is. This busy beetle is my soul, catching the sun on its black back and moisture on its belly, known to all creation, to its engenderer, and blessed by Him, granted life by Him – look, how my soul has wings of infinite delicacy. In your scarab casing are all my pygmies and all my mills of love and joy, the healing of my infirmities, the forgiveness of my sins.

Lord, you have put forth your hand and touched my eyes and opened them to the singleness of Your love which boils over in purity and peace and grace and life eternal. I praise you Lord, who knew me in my mother's womb, knew Marigold, knew Evie, knew Beatrice: Know us yet and cup us in Your redeeming hand.

In Ituri you would capture these tiny creatures for me, would you not, my wee folk, smoke them in a covered pot and make a breakfast for me. I have no fire, I have no pot, I have no breakfast. Yet I know where due east lies, or lay an hour or so ago. If I aim northwards from wherever I have got to, is there not a fair chance of meeting the road running west from Cogolin to where the villa stands?

My waterhole has proved no part of any stream, but a stagnant sump, perhaps an ancient iron-dig. I have yet to discern the tilt of the land or any alignment of the dry stream-beds in successive gullies and ravines. Meanwhile, tramping north, my feet take me to higher ground and undergrowth less dense.

Look, it is already nine o'clock and Maïté's Henri from Clare's household, wearing a vest, will be at Marseilles airport greeting Evie with the news that her old friend from university has been mislaid and the hunt is on. Or rather, Clare, you will already have tried to reach Evie by mobile phone just as soon as she will have landed, or failing Evie, Victor. You are competent at these things, Clare. Maybe you will have caught Evie before she boarded at Heathrow – *Evie – I'll not be at Marseilles to meet you. Simon's gone missing in the forest here. Failed to return last night. We're worried he's broken a leg, or simply hopelessly lost. Not like him, I know. There are search parties – locals who know the forest … Yes: he's got us worried sick.*

Maïté's Henri will drive them. It will take an hour. Victor, to be self-recognisable, must assume command. The villa itself will be hq for Cogolin gendarmerie's search-and-rescue teams. Maybe there'll be dogs working away, to the scent of my pyjamas: such pursuits are joy to dogs. This will be a minor branch of Cogolin's tourist industry: rescue teams amply rewarded in foreign currency for scouring the Massif for blundering hikers from northern Europe. Victor will come forward with a special treat for the first to spot me – a trip, perhaps, to London and dinner in the House of Lords for the lord-less French. Bishops of the C of E must be duly salvaged, and Victor is a Church Commissioner.

Evie, you will have turned pale at the phone call. 'Your old flame,' Victor will have consoled. 'Dearie me! We shall have to track him down … But you had a storm last night, the captain told us on the flight. *La tempête, n'est-ce pas? Le Mistral.*'

My lifted big-toenail slows my pace. It will take months to grow out black. I am somewhat weak.

Let body be mortified.

Breakfast at the villa will not have been as usual. The same fare but less expansively displayed. The same faces, but one missing leaving his smear of unquiet on all the others – on Fergie, Reggie, Charley, Julian, Sir Gunther, and with varying intensity on the ladies who will have rallied to Clare, absolving her for her choice of so daft a vagrant guest. I join you all my beloveds in pity for my disappearance, adding to all your woes, and in shame of my dereliction as the lover of your souls, as the *meister* that you deserve and need. For you too are no less unfindably lost than I, who should be not this egregious distraction but a light to guide you. Merger Fergie would be occupied with his devices for making money in a falling market and Chancery Charley with assessing whether an onset of devaluation will not enhance the value of a lawyer's standard fees, and Julian with watching his bullion scampering up. You are good citizens, my old buddies, my hearties – good enough and well enough brought up, contributing somehow to the weal. And you too Sir Gunther in your adoptive role, taking at face value what you judge to be most esteemed in the England of your adoption. I have no right to smile wryly at you. And as for Reggie, our multi-faceted multi-millionaire, amid this fuss and flurry over the missing Simon he'd partied with so gaily amid his pop-art murals at Worcester, you'd rather at this very moment be in search not of him but of a haven for this or that parcel of your off-shore wealth.

Each one of you has your stanchion of self-esteem and yours, Reggie is sheer money and the suave adroitness of your financial inventiveness. You and your current Gabby have just spent a few days aboard a friend's yacht moored in St Tropez bay which the financial storm has left unsunk, making you both bronzed more evenly than the rest of us. Your stanchion requires you not to be seen running scared before the maelstrom. You will already have seized today's English newspaper Victor and Evie will have picked up on the plane. You have no refuge from yourself, whether or not you find one for yourself. My prayer singles you out. You stay on top: that is what you're bred to do, what feeds your zest, keeps you sprightly. You have your fitness trainer (so you've mentioned), pop your dietary supplements, watch your physique, have toyed with countering the retreat of your hair by judicious implanting like that Italian politico who would stay on top in all departments including hair. I pray for you. Gabby says she likes you as you are since she, lithe divorcee, leather-skinned and ginny-voiced, must have herself liked as she is, needing her drinkie and her fag and in no sense evil either. To gratify your Gabby you have your own Mediterranean villa round the sea's corner in Catalonia where each of us is half-invited to join you when occasion suits, amid the crowded schedule of seasonal venues. The unexceptionable trick, Reggie, is only staying on top, which is where you are and which the abandonment of a brace of marriages not so much contradicts as endorses. That there were offspring from those evanescent unions might suggest a fleeting moment's expectation of permanence, but if there was pain you've cauterized the sore. 'Life's too short', isn't it, Reggie, in the vulgar codex, to dwell upon one's false moves. The candle's brief enough.

For you I pray. *Lord have mercy.*

Truly I am unsuited to return to the house-party I have disrupted. I am unsuited to share six days there with you, Evie, acting out a masque of acquaintance desiccated by the passage of time amid my Fergies, Reggies and Gabbies, Julians and Charleys and Sir Gunther and his very English Pauline with her quick wit and small-talk at this brink of the disappearance of the world-as-we-have-known-it.

God knows, the soul will out. Evie is of the soul, and soul has me here. If Evie and I are to re-encounter, it shall be in this forest; and here souls are stripped naked as ever bodies were for you and me, Evie.

My soul would be also thus with you here, my Lord, in your stormed church-forest, yours and mine, with our boars and my brilliant beetle of dazzling dark, our needle-shafts of brother sun, our sister wind, the hooped defiance of your trees, the gleaming leaves and riotous fungi, reversèd thunder, the incessant beauty of your presence.

Let us keep our innocence, Evie, and our Love undefiled. Now all is clear to me, Evie, as I watch my beetle in its pool of sun. At that terrible descent of the Eumenides upon us at Oxford, it seemed that to save ourselves we were to abandon the baby of our own making in mid-winter on a Theban mountainside. That infant's name, I tell you Evie, was Innocent. Ours was the pristine love that heaven makes, whose innocence was its validity, beyond all things mammon. This love belonged to the world in that you and I were in the world. To run out of innocence and see our love demeaned and traduced as was Abelard's and Paolo's was unbearable. The single compulsion, the vivific grail, named Innocence, has shaped my destiny. It is that cup of which Dante sipped with Beatrice. It is that which I was born with, which gripped me as a child at Rannoch, drew me into the precarious study of the Divine Comedy and the Beatrice of my discovery and to the altar of Christian faith and my mission with the Bambuti of the forest. In that grail love reposes, in it truth known as transcendent peace. It is a gift that Man alone may receive, in brilliant paradigm of human love. Look, look, this truth speaks joy. This is our ingot inheritance, from You. This grail. This cup.

Evie, Marigold: listen, listen. Person brings to person what You made, one-to-one. Hence our first commandment, loving You. Each of our beings and bodies and our creative flights are but brokers of the love that governs Your universe.

My ascent is steady here, as if I have stumbled upon a long-neglected track to draw me up … I scarcely have the stamina to keep at it. My legs are half-obedient, yet a capricious energy has taken possession of my will. *Ma lietament a me medesma indulgo / La cagion di mia sorte.* Joyously did Dante, too, yield to me the turn of his tale. For as the track rises, it is joined by another faint route that has climbed more steeply out of the ravine to my right. Once again I seem to be among random breccia of antique habitance and human workings, scarcely detectable and deeply overgrown, as if marooned folk had gone to ground up here, readmitted by the earth.

Is not sweet rest awaiting also me, Lord? Yet You urge me on. Here in ever higher ground the trees are spaced more openly and, more free of undergrowth. The forest's gloom is less. My hint of a track takes me round a knoll to the left, and looming beyond the trees no more than fifty strides ahead there comes into view what is unmistakably the dark high wall and turret of a stone-built church.

This cannot but be what Maïté spoke of, a mere ninety minutes' brisk excursion from the site of the villa so she said. It rises seventy feet amid its trees. Beyond, the forest continues to mount, and the glow of sky there speaks of some kind of summit, surely the summit's supreme pinnacle.

Drawing near, I see at once that the little church's roof has held intact, or is kept so by blind loyalty of surviving Christ-believers. I move round below the blank wall of the south side to where the apse should be. Is this not still your place, Lord, where once was praise and music? I would enter and offer prayer. I have reached this sudden testament, the metaphor of stone and tiles that once held and worked as prayer to be their vehicle and vector of truth which cannot deal in words written, spoken or even sung. The deconsecration has trapped truth, poised here on this highest place to await its ransom by me who has ascended by the route of a life to its remote forested eminence. Here the metaphor defiant in stone of a faith awaiting this very ransom I have brought and am, Simon Chance, priest and servant.

Here at this further end, cistus blooms where sun pours down, and the ground seems to have heaved in counter-sanctity to collapse the edifice where it once enclosed an altar. For your house here, Lord, at the upper end has been demolished and, thus truncated, the building re-assembled and sealed off with no sanctuary at all.

It is stripped of all claims to sanctity. Here is a low oak door let into the rebuilt wall. The door is locked. Can I enter?

I cannot.

This then my destination – where destiny has brought me, and I am awaited.

The only window, of plain glass, is small and high up in the turret wall that first met my eyes. I shall circuit the edifice. At that end that first met my eyes is a kind of niche or open-sided chimney in fashioned stone running the full height of the church and capped by a tricorn of tiles. Beneath this tricorn I can see a bell is hung, still on its axle. From the bell's cradle a cord dangles to a height of seven or eight metres from the flagstones where I stand. That bell could broadcast my presence and summon those who will be searching for me: my companions of the villa and my early life and now perhaps joined by Evie.

Am I man enough to scale this exterior chimney and sound the bell, and get back down again to earth?

No Bambuti would have been daunted by such a challenge. Bare-foot and bare-backed they would have braced the body between the chimney walls and mounted inch by inch by flexed shoulder muscles and flattened feet to the height of the bell's cord.

Do I dare? Is my body up to such a feat? To summon Evie?

Yet first I am drawn to ascend to whatever summit of forest may await beyond and above this rump of a church, perhaps to view from that eminence the massif's vast distances in all directions and even gather a clue to a route out to habitation and human presence.

By a precipitous ascent among thinning trees I have reached an open summit of bald rock. This pinnacle seems at my approach a place known to the kingdom of beasts, like the lair and citadel of a great cat, lithe, swift and streaked, a puma leaping there and unassailable. Or else, in previous times, a sacrificial platform for a pagan line of stone-flaking men. On my surmounting this venerated elevation my gaze is accorded sight of a created universe given which offers hope and declares release. The panorama of clefted forest spreads below me as far as any eagle's eye can see – to the south-east at twenty miles the apron of a misty sea.

Now I have turned to view north-west.

I am stunned. Here before me and below me some three to four miles distant a sight so familiar to my mind's eye comes in view that it must be playing me tricks.

Not so! No tricks. There, far down, beyond a sun-drenched vale stretches a sheen of still lake-water, and a shoreline of yellow rock or dune and exquisite verdancy that I have known since boyhood. Farther, and imprecisely, the delectable landscape bends away and vanishes beyond the reach of any eye amid its own bliss.

It is the terrestrial reality of my childish vision, the site of paradise, of which I was accorded precognition forty years ago!

I cannot credit this. I demand of myself if I have grown heady and deluded with hunger and exhaustion. Yet here below me without any doubt lies the half-distant vale and its placid lake that I was once vouchsafed, and here's the pain of my lifted toe-nail. It is all as real as the empty tomb, given to me this moment as if it all was awaiting my ascent.

I am entranced. This is where I should be, Lord, and where you have brought me out of small privation; it is where to make my daily orisons and pray my mantra of self-emptying. Surely it is for me to re-consecrate the church just beneath my summit, and refashion it a cross where memory may intersect with love.

This lofty precinct and its revelation were pre-ordained. That half-distant strath of delectation awaits me in the due hour.

And now? Now, it is well past noon. How they must be scouring for me! Evie herself among the searchers

Exhilarated, I begin my descent to the deformed church in its tilted grove. How did it come to be built? Maïté said that in past times these hills were dug for iron ore. Through some gesture of pious enthusiasm the place of worship must have been built for the labourers' salvation. Even yet this building must still be receiving a modicum of care.

Stripped of sanctity it belongs to the world of remnant men. So still do I; though I would re-consecrate this place. I can hardly transform myself into its anchorite, to hunt and gather here. Yet entering the glade, I already know it as holy. The high clean sun has set it aglow in perfect silence. Beneath my feet, from where the chancel would once have risen, it is as if the ground has turned over in its sleep and collapsed the artifice of worshipping man. I drop to my knees in sheer thanksgiving for the joy of love that I and all created life can give back to the Lord of Love. Here around me in our sanctuary of sunlight are all my fellow creatures, each leaf, stalk, blade and frond in their collective hush and whisper, and none but hath his noontide-hymn, each oak and thicket and black beetle doth know I AM.

In such certainty now, at the foot of this chimney below the bell I am to summon those who seek me, and summon Evie. I review how to reach the cord and sound the bell. The three-sided chimney has the width of a doorway. I shed socks and trainers. I shed my shirt. I attempt to brace myself horizontally for a perilous ascent. Theoretically it is possible. I am ready to lacerate my back and upper arms. What is a mere twenty feet of rock chimney to a young fit climber? I am neither young nor fit: I am elderly, and weak of muscle. I have ingenuity and will, and faith.

I begin upon an alternative posture, I replace my trainers, tightly laced, and using the rough-hewn stone of the building for grip I prop myself, facing down, diagonally across the chimney's walls. This fiercely strains the muscles of the arms and abdomen. Yet ascent is possible. I rise five feet and fall back to the ground. I begin anew.

Now my agility surprises me. A divine hand is lifting me. The strain on my arms and guts charges me. If I fall, this church will be re-consecrated by the blood of a priest. I am succeeding. I have the frayed cord in my teeth and, firmly braced, yank it. The bell sounds forth. I can go on sounding it by the movement of my head. My holy bell must be audible from a mile. I summon Evie. I summon irresistible love; she shall hear me first, she whose smile is not with teeth but only eyes, in secret, and in a tremor of the lip.

Listen to this bell above me! It is summoning more than searchers for a vagrant priest but all the unseen long-gone people of this massif, back to their sacred place. It is but a stump of a church, yet perched here in wild strain and pulling with my teeth with the rhythm of the bell's swing, I know that I am making it anew a place of worship. Here is the swell of its organ and the raising of the people's voices. Listen. *Out of the deep I have called unto You, O Lord. Lord, hear my voice.* I can hear the growl of the organ within. I can hear amid it the growl of my Bambuti's bass bamboos. Then what is this descending? – this ode of Jasper's threnody, this sublime motif of his mother's strings fluttering in octaves to redeem the tears which any life makes necessary; rhapsodic and redemptive, such being the very purpose of life's gift: that we should be *bought back*, brought back, out of the wail at our birth – be risked and ransomed, lost and found, Dives and Lazarus, re-bosomed from high. It is what my ears now hear, reversèd grief, the incanting of redemption heard and here acknowledged on behalf of every soul. I am poised so perilously beneath this primitive campanile. Within this granite space in its high forest the Holy Spirit is abroad and the sleeping Lord awoken by the astonishing role that it has raised me up to seize. All love is rendered one, and floods me, floods me.

My arms shudder at the weight of my body. And my mouth releases the cord for me to listen to the triumph of truth I have engendered in the people's throats. As I know His hands to have borne me up, so He will surely bring me down: there can be nothing to fear, I have pealed the truth. I allow my mouth once more to snatch and yank the bell-rope, and in the paean of praise I fly. O get me wings …

There are faces over me, voices. A figure looms upon me, bends and kisses my mouth. This is Love. It is a flame shooting through my body. On the instant I know the power of my limbs to be restored. I get to my feet in wonder; in joy I lean back against the wall of the deconsecrated church. And there are angels.

From the report submitted to L'Officier de Police Judiciare, Région de Cogolin, Var, by Maïté Duchamps, housekeeper, at Villa Les Maures.

We heard the sound of the bell when our group of five was still some fifteen minutes' tramp through the forest to the abandoned church of St Sulpice. We stopped to pick up the distant tolling. My companions were Mme Clare C—s, M. Walter Fawkes, Lord Goodenough and Lady Goodenough who had arrived that morning by plane from London. It was in M. Fawkes' presence that I recall telling the Bishop of the abandoned church I had been taken to as a child. M. Fawkes knew what sort of an invitation such a site would be to a man of God.

All the other search parties had been despatched in their allocated directions.

Lord and Lady Goodenough had arrived at the Villa Les Maures after the other parties had been despatched. Lord Goodenough had unpacked a green sweater with shoulder-patches. Lady Goodenough was wearing the same slacks and shirt she had worn for the flight from London.

We halted to listen to the bell. I said, 'C'est lui.'

I produced my whistle and blew it. There was no response. But the distant tolling was audible for a full minute. Then it paused.

After a few seconds it momentarily resumed.

Now we hurried on. I led the way. The track was a barely discernible but took us up its final ascent and the church came into view.

At the head of the company I exclaimed, 'Il est tombé.' I had seen the body instantly, twenty metres distant, at the foot of the niche in the church's western wall below the bell and its rope which reached only to six metres from the ground.

The Bishop lay crumpled on his side, naked above the waist, facing away from us, the upper arm flung forward across the flagstone. Blood oozed from the skull. The upper back was lacerated. A green shirt was to one side. Coming closer, we saw the mouth and eyes were open. We judged him dead. M. Fawkes muttered, 'Oh mon Dieu.'

There was no movement of breathing. Mme C—s was bending down as if to listen for a heartbeat. She shook her head. M. Fawkes repeated his muttering.

Lord Goodenough advised, 'Be careful moving him.' And then, 'In case his neck is broken.' Lady Goodenough beside him was evidently moved.

Mme C—s straightened up and said, 'I don't think he's breathing.' She seemed about to weep. She looked at Lady Goodenough, who was stock still. I saw the pallor on her. M. Fawkes had moved to the feet of his friend the Anglican, to gaze upon the body.

The other three (M. Fawkes being apart) in the dappled sunlight, were standing in a narrow triangle, half-facing one another, not knowing who should take the next action. The gash to the skull was entirely visible from where we stood. I now knelt beside the body.

I said, 'Il est mort, l'évêque,' and crossed myself.

M. Fawkes said to himself, 'How can this be?'

Lord Goodenough now addressed M. Fawkes. 'He was the father of my boy Gyles.'

This I did not understand.

But Lady Goodenough moved towards her husband. She placed her arms around his neck and buried her face upon his chest. Mme C—s laid a hand on each. In this manner they stood, locked together, each weeping without restraint.

May I recommend the replacement of the bell rope and the re-consecration of this church.

finis